Night
Hoops

Night Hoops

by Carl Deuker

Houghton Mifflin Company

Boston

The text of this book is set in 10.5 point Slimbach.

Library of Congress Cataloging-in-Publication Data

Deuker, Carl.
Night hoops / Carl Deuker.
p.   cm.
Summary: While trying to prove that he is good enough to play
on his high school's varsity basketball team, Nick must also
deal with his parents' divorce and the erratic behavior of a troubled
classmate who lives across the street.
ISBN 0-395-97936-6
[1. Basketball—Fiction. 2. Divorce—Fiction. 3. Behavior—Fiction.
4. Friendship—Fiction.] I. Title.
PZ7.D493 Ni   2000
[Fic]—dc21
99-047882

Manufactured in the United States of America
QUM   10 9 8 7 6 5 4

For Anne and Marian;
and for Ratty, Striper, Gigi, Phantom, and Trixie

The author would also like to thank Ann Rider,
the editor of this book, for her support and advice.

Part
One

Chapter 1 Against the fast break, you have to stop the ball. That's rule number one, even if it's Trent Dawson, eyes wild, who's barreling down the lane at you, and even if it's just a summer pick-up game. You've still got to suck it up and do it. So I challenged him, holding my position, feet set.

With the advantage in numbers he had, a simple bounce pass would have given one of his teammates the easy two points. Trent knew that, because he was a player. Or he could have been a player, if he ever played right. But Trent Dawson never did anything right.

Instead of passing off, he crashed right into me, planting his knee into my chest. I toppled backwards, and he came down hard on top of me. My head smacked the asphalt just as the ball rolled in. "That was a charge," I yelled, still pinned under him. "The basket doesn't count."

His hand came right back to my face, his fingers squeezing my cheeks and almost gouging my eyes. "No way, Abbott. No way."

1

Every guy on the court knew he was cheating, but nobody backed me. I can't blame them, because the one thing worse than having Trent Dawson squeeze your face would be to have him pound it to a bloody pulp. And he'd do it, too. He'd do it and he'd enjoy it.

"Take the points," I sputtered, pushing his hand away, "but you fouled me and you know it."

He grinned as he climbed off me. It was his way of letting me know that he *did* know it.

The game ended in a typical Dawson way. We were playing to twenty. My team had the ball with the score tied at eighteen when Trent's older brother Zack showed up. Trent is bad news, but Zack is worse, both meaner and crazier. Word is that he has a gun that he stole from one of his mother's many, many boyfriends.

"Hey, Trent. Let's go," he shouted from across the court.

Immediately, without so much as a "Good game" or a "See you later," Trent was gone, leaving the rest of us with sweat dripping down our faces and backs, our mouths hanging open. "What a total jerk," one of the guys said, but not until Trent was out of earshot.

The joke is that last year, when Trent first moved into the rental house across the street from us, I was keyed up about it. A guy my age, who looked pretty athletic — it was perfect. Dad knew, though. He never liked the Dawsons. "Freeloaders" is what he called them, because they were on welfare. "There'll be trouble. Mark my words."

Mom, who is a nurse at the county hospital and sees a lot

of poor people, defended them. "Not having money doesn't make you a criminal."

Dad grinned. "Just wait. In six months you'll be singing a different tune."

Normally Mom isn't all that outgoing, but she made a point of welcoming Ericka Dawson to the neighborhood, calling out "hello" to her in the morning and encouraging me to do stuff with Trent.

But Dad turned out to be right. On our block everybody mows the lawn, plants flowers, and picks up stray bits of trash. People wave to their neighbors, keep their music down, and drive slowly, at least until they hit the main streets.

It didn't take long to see that Ericka Dawson was different. She let the lawn and flower beds go. Her front porch became a garbage heap, and if anything broke, it stayed broken. She had people over all the time, and they partied late and loud. Strange cars and motorcycles were always roaring up and down our block.

When the Dawsons moved in, the inside of the house had been clean and neat. Within three months the place was a total dump, and I mean total. I still remember the first time I was inside that house. Trent had me over to play pool on what turned out to be an undersized table, really just a toy, that one of his mother's boyfriends had given him.

The pool table was upstairs in his room. To reach it, we had to walk through the house. Newspapers, empty pizza boxes, and beer bottles were strewn around the living room floor and on the sofa. Cigarette butts spilled out of cups and off plates onto the tables and carpet. Plates crusty with dried food sat on top of the television set, which was on, the volume full blast. "What are you looking at?" Trent said when he caught me staring.

I was glad to make it to his room, but five minutes later his mother came upstairs. "Go home," she ordered, just like that, no explanation at all. I stood for a second, stunned. "You want me to draw you a picture?" she snapped. "Go home."

As I left I spotted a policeman standing in the kitchen, and the next day Dad found out that Zack had been caught stealing beer at Albertson's.

That was when Mom gave me the word: "Nick, stay out of that house. If Trent invites you over, you make some excuse. You understand?" Dad didn't have to say anything. His smile said it all.

Chapter 2 "Let's pick new teams," I said, once Trent had walked off the court that afternoon, but Leo Devencenzi grabbed his sweatshirt and slung it over his shoulder. "I'm going home, Nick," he said, and one by one the other guys followed until I was alone.

I shot around for a while, but finally there was nothing for me to do but go home, too. It was a Saturday, so Dad was around. I thought maybe I could get him to shoot with me, but when I opened the front door I heard him arguing with Mom. Right away I knew they were arguing about my older brother Scott.

You look at pictures of Dad when he was seventeen, and he looks exactly like Scott. Same brown hair and gray eyes, same thin lips and straight nose, same broad shoulders and long arms.

Dad was a three-year letterman in basketball, power forward. As a junior he'd had feelers from some major colleges. But in his senior year his coach told him to work on his passing and rebounding, and not to worry about scoring. He did what his coach said, only it didn't pay off. His rebounds and assists went up a little, but his points per game dropped a lot. College coaches stopped calling. I'm not sure his grades were all that hot either. He played at a junior college for a year, and then he quit school and basketball entirely. Now he's a machinist at the Boeing plant in Seattle. He makes decent money, but he's always saying how he should have gone further and done more.

What he means is that Scott should go further and do more. It's hard to disagree. Scott has every trait you look for in a basketball player. He's big, strong, and fast, with soft hands and a nice touch from fifteen feet and in. But he doesn't bleed basketball, not the way I do.

For the last two years he's made varsity at Bothell High. But Darren Carver has been the star, and Scott has been buried at the end of the bench. He plays a minute or two at the end of the quarters to give the starters a rest, and he's on the court if the game is a blowout, but he never plays the final minutes of a close game.

That eats at Dad. For as long as I can remember he has been after Scott to practice more. "Carver doesn't have more talent than you. You could do everything he does, if you worked at your game."

Scott nods and says the right things, but he prefers tooting away on his trumpet to walking twenty minutes to the basketball courts at Canyon Park Junior High. "They're too far away," he says if I ask him. Or: "It's too hot." Or: "It's too cold." Sorry excuses, and he uses them all the time. They make me mad, but they make Dad furious.

When I stepped inside the house that day, Dad was shouting so loud that he didn't hear me come in. I always get this huge lump in my throat when he screams at Mom. I feel as if there's something I should do to make him stop, but I don't know what. So I don't do anything; I can't talk or even move.

They were in the kitchen. Mom was staring out the window into the back yard, a cup of tea in her hand, looking cool and composed, though I'd heard enough of their arguments to know that if he pushed her hard enough, she'd get right in his face. Dad was pacing back and forth, swinging his arms around, as though he wanted to grab hold of something and crush it.

"It makes me sick to see him waste his talent," Dad was saying. "And it makes me even sicker to see you encourage him."

Mom said something I couldn't hear.

He wheeled on her. "You're not talking about that trumpet, are you?"

Again, she spoke so softly I didn't hear. But whatever she

said, Dad was having none of it. "Yeah, well, Nick shouldn't be there either. You know who hangs out there? Do you? Gang wannabes. Zack Dawson and Trent Dawson and that whole crew."

Mom's voice rose so that I could hear. "You are not going to use the Dawson boys as an excuse to rip out my rose garden."

"*Your* garden," Dad scoffed. "I don't suppose it has ever occurred to you that the back yard belongs to all of us."

She set her cup down hard on the kitchen counter. Her eyes fixed him. "Matthew, no basketball court. How many times do I have to say it? No. No. No. And that's final."

He laughed. "Oh, it's final, is it? Who do you think you are, the Queen of England? And how do you plan on ..."

Mom nodded toward me.

Dad's head jerked around. "How long have you been standing there, Nick?"

"I just came in," I stammered.

Dad's eyes honed in on me. "Nobody likes a sneak."

"I wasn't sneaking. I just this second opened the door."

He stared a moment longer. "Your mother and I are having a private conversation. You can go upstairs, downstairs, or outside, but you can't stand there."

"It's okay," Mom contradicted. "This conversation is over. Come in and sit down, Nick. Are you hungry? I'll make you something."

After that argument my parents went into what Scott calls their *polite phase.* They only talked to each other at mealtimes, and then only to ask for bread or mustard or potatoes. Every sentence began with *Please* and ended with *Thank you,* but their voices were colder than the pitcher of ice water on the table.

Chapter 3 It was a Monday. We'd finished breakfast. Scott was downstairs playing the trumpet while Mom and Dad were getting ready for work. I was sprawled out on the sofa in the front room, half reading the sports page and half looking out the window, when I saw Ericka Dawson's new boyfriend cross the street and head toward our house. Mom caught me looking out the window, so she looked too. "I wonder what he wants," she said.

Dad came from the kitchen, sipping a cup of coffee. "Who?"

"Ericka's latest is headed this way," Mom answered.

"I'll talk to him," Dad said. "I asked him to come."

Mom looked confused. "You asked him to come? Why?"

Instead of answering, he opened the front door and stepped onto the porch. "Good morning!" he called out. Then he motioned with his arm. "Right through that gate." The two of them disappeared around the corner to the back yard.

I looked to Mom. Her eyes had an intensity that scared me. She turned and went back to the kitchen, yanking the door shut behind her.

Scott heard the loud bang and came upstairs, trumpet in hand. "Something going on?" he asked, looking at the closed kitchen door.

"I'm not sure, but I think Dad is putting in a basketball court in the back."

"Really? Mom's letting him take out her rose garden?"

"I don't think she wants him to, but he's doing it anyway."

Scott shook his head. "Oh, man. And I was hoping things would get back to normal around here." He scowled, then went back downstairs.

I slipped out the front door and walked around back. When I caught up to Dad, he was standing in front of the circular rose bed. Using both hands, he was holding up a big piece of butcher paper so whatever-his-name-was could see it. The dark-eyed man, who was wearing a cut-off sweatshirt and jeans, asked some questions. After Dad answered, he turned to me.

"I'm going inside to talk to your mom, and then I'll be off to work. You can help if you want. Just don't get in Mr. Clay's way." He winked. "You and Scott are going to like this. You're going to like it a lot."

Once Dad had disappeared into the house, I turned back to Mr. Clay. In a way he was like all of Ericka Dawson's boyfriends. You could see from the deep lines in his face that he'd smoked too much and drank too much. The skull-and-crossbones tattoo on his forearm told the same story. But there was something different about him, something that made me want to stay.

"I'm Steve," he said, sticking out his hand.

"Nick Abbott," I answered, shaking it.

"I know. Trent has talked about you."

I was stunned. "Trent talks about me? What's he say?"

Steve Clay shrugged. "He says you're a good—"

Just then, from inside the house, we heard Mom scream at Dad. I felt myself go red in the face as Dad yelled back at her. Then they were both shouting. Finally a door was slammed; then another one. There was a short pause before Dad's truck started up. I could hear him rev the engine, slam the transmission into gear, and roar off.

A dog barked, breaking the spell that had come over both of us. Steve Clay hefted the shovel in his hand. "Well, I'd better get to work. Your dad isn't paying me to stand here talking, much as I wish he would."

That was a confusing day. I knew how much Mom loved her rose garden, how much time she spent in the summer pruning and raking and checking for black spot and aphids. Seeing bush after bush uprooted and tossed onto the lawn as if they were so much junk made me sick to my stomach. But I wanted that basketball court, too. As it slowly came into existence, I found myself caring less about the rose garden or Mom.

It took all day for Steve Clay to dig out the bushes and the lawn, and that was with me helping him, holding the tape measure and staking out lines. He was a real perfectionist. If Dad's plans called for twenty-six feet, he made it twenty-six feet—not an inch more and not an inch less. Sometimes I'd measure something, and be off by six inches or so. I couldn't see how a couple of inches one way or the other could matter, but he'd grimace whenever he discovered an error, and then he'd go back and fix it. After my third or fourth mistake he leaned against his shovel. "If you'd go slower, we'd get finished faster."

Once we had the bushes out and the outline of the court complete, Steve Clay spent another half hour yanking out stray bits of sod and pulling up roots he'd missed. "Well, that does it for me today," he said.

After he left, I moved around on that patch of bare dirt pretending to dribble and shoot an imaginary basketball at an imaginary hoop. "What are you doing, Nick?" Scott called down to me from his upstairs window.

"Nothing," I said, humiliated at being caught acting like a little kid. I motioned to the dirt. "Isn't this going to be great?"

"Sure. But I wouldn't want to be Dad tonight."

For dinner we had Thai food delivered. Mom picked at her meal, and didn't speak at all until the dinner was about over. Then she looked at Scott and me. "Are you happy about the basketball court?"

I nodded. So did Scott.

"Good," she said, forcing herself to smile. "That's something."

Dad tried to take her hand. "Caroline, there's still room for a little garden over by the camellias. I'll buy you new roses, put down some compost and peat moss, and you can start fresh."

She pulled away from his touch. "I don't want new roses; I don't want to start fresh. So please, Matthew, don't do anything more. You've done quite enough, thank you."

Dad leaned back in his chair. I could hear him breathing, slow and deep like some dangerous animal.

The next morning an old guy showed up, a cigarette dangling from his lip, a two-day stubble on his face. He was a retired contractor, and with Dad and Steve Clay's help, he was going to finish the job.

It was strange watching the three of them work together. I'm used to Dad being in charge, knowing what to do, giving directions. But with this old guy he was just a helper. Even Steve Clay knew more than Dad did.

The three of them rolled the earth smooth, laid down sand and dirt, rolled it again, measured it again, built wood frames for the concrete, hammered some more, rolled some more. By the end of the day, the scar of earth that had been our yard was as smooth as the infield on a baseball diamond. "The cement mixer will be here tomorrow morning around nine," the old guy said. Then he turned to me. "In a few days, you are going to be the proud owner of the best basketball court in Bothell."

Chapter 4 Once the court was in, I didn't go up to
Canyon Park Junior High. If the games there had been good, I might have, but too many of them were ruined by Trent Dawson. It was easier to shoot around in the back yard, especially since I had Scott to play against. He practiced his trumpet as much as ever, maybe even more. But when he was finished practicing, he came out and shot hoops with me.

When Dad came home from work, he would ask if we'd played ball during the day, and when we said we had, he'd look over at Mom with an *I told you so* on his face.

After dinner the three of us would go out and shoot some

more. Dad was always looking to go one-on-one against Scott. "You think you can stop your old man?" he'd say.

Scott would only half try, and Dad would barrel by him for the hoop. "Is that the best you can do?"

I'd step up. "Try to drive on me," I'd say. And sometimes Dad would. But he never took me seriously, never came at me the way he went after Scott. No matter what I did or how well I did it, Scott came first.

Take last season. I'd been the starting point guard on Canyon Park Junior High's team, and I was good, leading the team in scoring and assists. But my games were on the same day as Scott's. If Dad showed up for mine, it was only for a few minutes. He'd shout out that I should play hard and tough, and then he'd be off to Bothell High to watch Scott. I understand why he did it. Why watch a junior high game when there's a high school game going on? Still, I didn't much like seeing his back as he left the gym.

While our court was new, we mainly played "Horse" and "Twenty-one" and "Bump." But little by little, and so slowly I could never say when it started, Dad began riding Scott, hectoring him to work on his shot, his rebounding, his dribbling, his passing. Scott would balk. "Can't we just shoot around?" he asked more than once.

One day, after Scott missed a jump shot from the corner, Dad rebounded the ball and wheeled on him. "How many times have I told you to get some arc on your shot?"

Scott didn't answer.

"How many? Two? Six? Six hundred?"

Scott still said nothing.

His silence made Dad seethe. "Since that question is too hard for you, maybe you can answer this one. Do you plan on playing varsity basketball this year? Or are you going to do that jazz band thing I hear you whispering about with your mom all the time?"

I knew Scott had been toying with the idea of quitting the basketball team so he could play with the jazz band year-round, and that Mom was all for it. But I didn't think Dad knew.

"I'll probably play basketball again."

"You'll *probably* play," Dad mimicked. "And how many minutes do you think you'll probably play? Or does that matter to you?"

Scott didn't answer, but I could see his jaws grinding.

"Listen, and listen good," Dad said at last. "I need to know what the score is with you. If you're not serious about basketball, fine. I won't waste my time trying to teach you anything. But if you're going to try to make something of yourself on the court, something other than a third-string bench-warming senior, then it's time to get busy. So what's it going to be? Do you want to be a player, or don't you?"

Scott took a deep breath, exhaled. "I want to be a player," he said, almost in a whisper.

"I didn't hear you," Dad said sharply.

"I want to be a player," Scott repeated, this time loud and clear and angry.

"So that means you're making a commitment."

"Yeah."

"Not a half commitment. A commitment. No quitting."

"I'm no quitter," Scott snapped.

For a moment the two of them glared at one another like boxers before a fight, and they looked so much alike it was scary. Dad's face relaxed ever so slightly. "All right," he said, "since you're making a commitment to me, I'll make a commitment to you. I promise to teach you everything I know about basketball." He paused. "You could be good, Scott. You could be very, very good."

After that Dad was like a drill sergeant. He'd have Scott practice passing, dribbling, shooting. Once he was satisfied with Scott's basic skills, he moved on to more complicated lessons: footwork on defense, blocking out on rebounds, posting up on offense.

Scott burned to prove Dad was wrong. You could see him trying, trying. But he couldn't keep up his intensity. He could play his trumpet for hours and never even notice time. But he wasn't that way on the basketball court.

When Scott started to slack off, Dad would ride him. "What about that commitment? I thought you made a promise." Then, for a while, Scott would play with fire again. But only for a while.

Me? I was the other guy. Dad would take me by the shoulders and move me to a spot and tell me what to do. Scott would practice shooting over me or driving around me, blocking me off the backboard or stuffing my shots. Not much fun. Some days I wished that Dad had never built the court. Bad as those games at Canyon Park Junior High had been, at least they were *my* games.

Chapter 5 Scott and I were playing horse one afternoon toward the end of July when Darren Carver showed up at the back fence, Matt Markey and Carlos Fabroa trailing behind him.

Carver was more than the best basketball player at Bothell High. He was the class president, the most popular with girls, an A student. He'd never come to our house before, and it didn't take a rocket scientist to figure out why he'd come now. "I heard you put in a new basketball court," he said, leaning over the fence and staring at it as if it were some gorgeous girl.

"Sure did," Scott answered. "Come on back. We can play some." As Darren pushed the gate open, Scott turned to me. "Beat it, Nick."

I looked at him, not believing what I'd heard.

"Get lost!" His voice was commanding.

"But I want to play."

"Well, you can't."

Furious, I stormed up to my room and flung myself onto my bed. I lay there, arms folded across my chest, listening to the basketball bouncing and Scott and his friends laughing. I tried to tune them out, but I couldn't. At last I slipped over to the window and peered down onto the court.

They were playing a two-on-two game. Scott was matched up against Carver. I wanted Carver to eat him up, but all the stuff Dad had taught Scott was paying off. He kept good position on defense and he blocked Carver off the boards. On offense Scott's jump shot was falling, and if Carver came up and tried to guard him tight, he'd give him an up-fake and then drive to the hoop.

But slowly things changed. As fatigue set in, Scott and Matt and Carlos started playing lazy. They'd throw up long jumpers, back off on defense. They stopped blocking out on rebounds, stopped hustling after loose balls.

Not Carver. The longer they played, the harder he scrapped. More and more of the rebounds and the loose balls ended up in his hands. He kept taking high-percentage shots, and he kept sinking them. During the first ten minutes, Scott had played Carver even up. For the last half hour, Carver dominated him.

You've got to want it more than the guy you're playing. I thought when Dad said that he was talking about pumping yourself up for the big game or the big quarter or even the big shot. But watching Carver made me realize "wanting it" means playing every second of every game as if it's the biggest moment in the biggest game of your life. You can't turn "wanting it" off and on. It's in you, or it isn't. It was in Darren Carver, but not in Scott. I had to find out if it was in me.

Chapter 6 The next day, after Mom and Dad had gone to work and Scott had finished practicing his trumpet, I challenged him to go one-on-one. He shook his head. "Carver's coming by."

"It'll be a good warm-up."

He considered for a while. "Okay."

Once we were on the court, I pushed harder. "Let's really play. Winners outs, game to eleven, score by ones. No goofing around."

He looked at me, a quizzical look on his face. "You sound like Dad."

"Come on," I said.

"I'll whip you."

And he did. He took me 11–3 and 11–4, outrebounding me and muscling up short jumpers and lay-ins. I'd have played a third game, but Carver and the other guys showed up, and Scott shooed me away.

I challenged him again the next day, and every day. Our games didn't change much. I wasn't big enough to mix it up with him inside, and I couldn't knock down enough outside shots to put a scare into him. The best I could do was 11–7, and I came that close only a couple of times.

When I was alone, I worked on my outside shot, figuring that to beat him I had to hit everything. But the next day Scott would crush me again, and I'd be back to square one.

Then came another afternoon when I was chased upstairs so Scott could play with Carver and his buddies. As I stood at my window watching their game, the reason I was losing to Scott suddenly hit me. Carver was a couple of inches shorter than Scott, but he still took the ball inside, using his quickness and his moves to score, making Scott defend the whole court.

That's not how I'd been playing. I'd given up the inside game, figuring I had no chance. Since I wasn't pushing the ball inside, Scott was all over me outside, hurrying my shots and forcing me farther and farther out.

The next morning I challenged Scott again. It was just another game to him, at least in the beginning. But early on he found out that I was done heaving up twenty-footers. I moved my game inside. I took a few elbows, and I cut my knees up when he knocked me to the cement. But the games were tighter, 11–8 and 11–9. And I dished out a little punishment, too.

"Let's play one more," I said after I'd lost the second game. Scott shook his head.

"Why not? Afraid you're going to lose?"

"Don't be stupid. You can't beat me."

"You're scared to play because you know I will."

I was trash-talking him, though I didn't plan it. And it worked. "All right, Nick. You want a lesson; you'll get a lesson."

He came out on fire, nailing his first three jumpers. "I thought you were going to eat me up," he jeered after his third shot went down.

"I am," I shot back. "You'll see." He laughed, then took one dribble, raised, and drained another jumper to go up 4–0.

I was down 6–0 before Scott missed and I touched the ball for the first time. I took it to the corner, and he was slow getting out to cover me. Instead of going up for the jumper, I drove to the hoop and kissed the lay-in off the backboard. 6–1.

He didn't guard me tight on my next bucket either, a little eight-footer I swished after he went for a head fake. On my next possession I got off another good shot, an uncontested pull-up fifteen-footer that missed off the back rim. Scott rebounded, took the ball back, and nailed a long set shot, pushing the score to 7–2.

Five buckets is a big lead, but every one of his scores had come from outside. Lazy man hoops. He thought he could win easily; I knew I'd have to work.

I stuck a hand right up in his face on his next shot, another long-range bomb that fell short. I was on the rebound like a hawk. I took the ball back, then worked my dribble in close, finally blowing by him with a crossover dribble for a lay-in.

That's how the rest of the game went—Scott casting off long jumpers while I scored my points in the key. I closed to 8–5, then 9–8. He missed a twelve-footer, I shagged the rebound, raced to the corner and—for the first time—let an outside shot go. Nothing but net! We were tied.

He grabbed the ball as it went through the net and bounced it to me. I faked another long jumper. He lunged out to try to block it, and I drove past him for my tenth hoop.

Scott carried the ball out and shoved it into my gut, trying to intimidate me. But I wasn't backing down.

He crouched low. I swung the ball in front of him, tempting him. Finally he swiped at it, but his hands were too slow. As his body moved forward, I took two hard dribbles to the left. He was a half-step behind me, and when I pulled up for the jumper, he stumbled a little. I had a good look at the hoop, and knocked down a twelve-footer for the victory. "Yes!" I shouted, making a fist and pumping it. "Yes! Yes! Yes!"

I'm not going to say I won every game after that. But I won

more than my share. Sometimes down at Golden Gardens, you can actually see the tide come in, see each wave claiming more and more of the beach. I was like those waves. Every day I felt my game growing stronger. Scott could push me aside when his buddies arrived, but when tryouts came, there'd be no sending me to my room.

Chapter 7 Then it was September and school. I thought I'd be going in with Scott, but he had band during zero period, and I didn't start until an hour after that. So I was on my own.

My last year at Canyon Park Junior High I'd pretty much had the run of the school. All ninth graders did. We ate lunch up on a patch of grass that we called the ninth-grade island. Unless there was a fight or something, not even teachers ventured there. In the school hallways, the little seventh-grade girls looked up at us as if we were gods, while the seventh-grade boys—the "sevies"—cleared a path for us. If we barked at them even a little, a terror-stricken look would come to their faces as if they were afraid we were going to wait for them after school and then chop them up into little pieces with a hatchet.

In the halls of Bothell High that first day, my world was suddenly upside-down. I was the little kid; the senior guys, especially the football players, towered over me. I found myself hugging the walls, nervously moving out of the way for them, praying that no linebacker would pick me out and start riding me the way some guys at Canyon Park had ridden seventh graders, making their lives hell for a year.

It wasn't just fear of being tortured that made Bothell different. At the junior high most of the girls looked like little kids; here lots of them looked like grown women. And the school was huge compared to Canyon Park. I had a class in Room 303, then my next class was in 107, and I finished the day with geometry in 705—which turned out to be a portable behind the gym.

Still, all that stuff was minor compared to the biggest problem: Trent Dawson. He was in my English class, my gym class, and my geometry class. We had the same lunch period, too. Every time I turned around, he was there.

And he was no different. Nobody fools around on the first day at a new school. Nobody except Trent. He saved his best—or worst—for last. He was late for geometry, talked while Mrs. Glandon was giving us the rundown on her rules, and on his way to the water fountain in the back of the room, he knocked the books off three kids' desks. When Devin Klein told him to cut it out, Trent stuck his face right up in Devin's and sneered: "Yeah, and what are you going to do about it?"

The walk home takes about thirty minutes. For the first fifteen I replayed the day in my mind. But once I reached my own block, my thoughts turned to basketball. I hoped I could get Scott to play, even if it was just horse. As I opened the front door I heard the trumpet coming from the downstairs den. I walked to the doorway. "You want to shoot some hoops?"

"No," came the answer.

"Why not?" I asked as I headed down, but before I reached

the bottom step I knew the reason. Sitting next to Scott on the sofa, clarinet in hand, was Katya Ushakov, back from her summer vacation in Russia.

Mom had met the Ushakovs at the grocery store a couple of years earlier. They'd come to America after the Soviet Union had broken up. Both of Katya's parents played for the Seattle Symphony. Every time you walked by their house, you'd hear music leaking out the windows and doors.

Katya's brother Michael had been in some of my classes at Canyon Park. They hardly seemed as if they could be brother and sister. She was beautiful, long and lanky, with red-blonde hair and blue eyes. She spoke English with an accent that made her even more attractive. Michael was dark, had little pig's eyes, and was so fat his flesh jiggled when he walked. When he talked to you, he stuck his face right up into yours, so close you could see the yellow on his teeth and smell the garlic on his breath.

For months he did terrible in school, but everybody figured it was because he didn't know English very well. Then one day in the cafeteria Trent called him a "retard." That got a laugh, so after that Trent ridiculed him all the time, especially after school, when no adults were around. On weekends Zack would join in. They'd follow Michael down the street, taunting him, "Michael, buddy, you need a bra? There's a sale at K mart."

This went on for a couple of months, until one day Michael was gone from school. Somehow we heard that he'd been transferred to Sherwood, which is a school for kids who can't learn in a regular class. But he wasn't gone from the neigh-borhood. The symphony's performances were at night, and that's when he'd wander around singing songs in Russian or feeding the ducks along the Burke-Gilman bike trail. Seeing him out at night worried Mom. "I don't like it," she'd say. "I don't like it at all."

"Don't worry. Bothell's safe," Dad would answer. "Besides, what can the Ushakovs do? They've got to work."

That afternoon I said hello to Katya, and then asked her about Michael. "He's okay," she replied in a way that made it clear he wasn't okay at all. "You should come by, Nick. He'd love to see you."

"I will. Once school settles down."

She nodded, but I knew she didn't believe me, and for good reason. Feeling guilty, I turned to Scott. "How long are you going to practice?"

He laughed. "Every spare minute I've got."

"Oh," I said. As soon as I left, they started playing again, and their music followed me to the back yard.

I had the basketball court to myself, but for a while all I could hear was their music. I thought about how angry Dad would be if he came home day after day and found Scott playing the trumpet. Then I pictured Mom, and how she'd take Scott's side, and how they'd all argue, and my head started to pound.

Basketball. That's what matters, I thought, shaking my head. I practiced dribbling with my left hand and then my right, behind my back, between my legs, crossovers, stutter steps. I practiced shooting pull-up jumpers and finger rolls, sweeping hooks and reverse lay-ins. I practiced my defensive footwork and blocking out on rebounds. I practiced that day and every day, the rhythm of my basketball nearly, but not quite, drowning out Scott's trumpet and Katya's clarinet.

While I shot around, first Mom and then Dad, would come home from work. Mom would wave and go inside to make dinner. Dad would shoot a hoop or two, maybe even play a little horse. And every day he'd ask the same question. "Did your brother practice at all?"

Every day I'd shake my head, and his eyes would darken.

Toward the end of September Dad was injured at work. A forklift driver started to lose a bunch of boxes, and when Dad grabbed for them his fingers were squashed. It was no big deal, nothing broken, but his left hand was so swollen the doctor told him to stay home for a couple of days.

When I returned from school that first afternoon, he was playing ball in the back yard. That didn't surprise me; puffy fingers weren't going to keep him down. What did surprise me was seeing Scott on the court with him. Katya was sitting on the back stairs, clarinet in hand, a bored look on her face. I sat down next to her to watch their game.

They were going one-on-one, and they were playing hard. Even with his swollen hand, Dad was crushing Scott. He'd post Scott up and shoot over him. If he missed he'd crash the boards, grab the rebound, and put up another shot. Power basketball, and Scott couldn't stop him.

Once Dad scored his eleventh point, Scott started off the

court. "Where you going?" Dad asked, a sharp edge to his voice.

Scott wheeled around, frustration on his face. "Like I've been telling you for the last half hour, I've got to practice. That's why Katya's here, you know."

"Yeah?" Dad said. "Well, Katya can wait a few more minutes. I want to see you play Nick."

"Why?"

"Because I want to. Is that so much to ask?"

Scott gave Katya a look, sighed loudly, then turned to Dad. "One game?"

Dad nodded.

"And then I'm done."

"Then you're done."

Scott looked to me. "All right, Nick. Let's play."

I thought I'd win easily, that Scott would roll over to get the game finished so he could play his trumpet. I'd forgotten that Katya was watching.

In the beginning I think he forgot too. I scored the first three buckets, two on pull-up jumpers and one on a lay-in. But after the third hoop Katya called out, "Come on, Scott!" and I knew he was coming after me.

It was on the boards that he did it. He was taller than I was by four inches, and without a ref to call over-the-back fouls, he could pound away inside. He did to me exactly what Dad had done to him. A couple of times he bodied me right off the court.

Down 9–6, I backed up a step and sunk a long jumper. He

shook his head. "Pure luck," he grumbled, but I swished another one, and then a third to tie it up.

That brought him right out on me, so close I could smell his sweat. I drove hard down the right side of the lane, then went behind the back and scooped up a little left-handed running hook that dropped. Score: 10–9, my lead. One more basket and I had him.

Again he guarded me tight, and again I drove the lane. Only this time I pulled up for the jump shot. He stayed with me though, and he swatted the ball out of the air. The ball was headed out of bounds, and it would have been my possession, but I hustled after it anyway, hustled because that's the way you win.

Scott watched me, not realizing what I was doing. So when I did grab the ball just before it went out-of-bounds, I was in the clear, so open in fact that I was afraid I'd choke the shot. I dribbled once to get some rhythm. Scott flew at me then, but he was way too late. I pulled the trigger. The ball soared high, tracing a beautiful rainbow, then fell out of the air, down and through. I'd beaten him.

As soon as the ball whistled through the net, Scott headed off the court. "You quitting?" Dad asked him, incredulous.

Scott didn't answer. Dad followed behind him as he headed up the back steps. "I don't understand you. Nick beats you in front of your girlfriend, and you don't even want a rematch."

Scott turned on him, his face contorted with anger. "What is it you want from me, Dad? What is it? You want me to be the big basketball star you never were. Is that it? Well, I'm not going to be. Got that? I'm not going to be. Maybe Nick will be, but I won't. So spend your time with him, and leave me alone."

The back door opened and Mom stepped out. I hadn't known she was home. I don't think Scott or Dad had known either. "What is all the screaming about?" she demanded, looking from Scott to Dad.

No one said anything. Scott looked at Dad, then turned to Katya. "Come on. Let's go downstairs."

"You're a quitter," Dad called after him. "You hear me! A quitter."

Mom stepped aside as Scott, red-faced with rage, stormed by her into the house. Katya followed him, her face pasty white. I stood on the court, holding the ball, looking from Mom to Dad and then back again to Mom. She was at the top of the stairs, her whole body quivering with fury, glaring at Dad. "What are you looking at?" he asked scornfully.

She studied him for a long time. "I don't know anymore. I just don't know." Then she went back inside the house, the door quietly clicking closed behind her.

Both Dad and I stared at the closed door for a while, almost as if we were in a trance. Then all at once he turned to me. "What do you say, Nick? You want to play some?"

Chapter 8 I heard the voices after midnight. At first it was the way it usually was, the low urgent tones, Dad louder than Mom. Then came the screaming, screaming like I'd

never heard before. Scott's door opened. We stood side-by-side at the top of the stairs and listened.

"Why does he have to play basketball? Will you tell me that? It's perfectly clear he likes music more. Is that so awful?"

"Get a clue. How many times do I have to tell you this? It isn't music he likes; it's Katya Ushakov's body. And you know what he wants to do with her—or should I say *to* her—as well as I do."

There was a long pause. "You've got a filthy mind, Matthew, but that doesn't mean Scott does."

"Every boy has a filthy mind, Caroline," Dad said. "That's one of the many things that you don't know about boys."

"I'll tell you one thing I do know," Mom shot back. "I do know how to talk to my son. He doesn't look at me with hatred in his eyes. At least not yet. But if you don't back off, he'll end up hating both of us. You're poisoning this house."

The laugh again. "So now I'm poisoning the house! If I'm so awful, I'm surprised you still want me around."

"Who says I do?"

It was as if a blast of icy air had filled every corner of the house. Mom's voice was different than I'd ever heard it, dark somehow.

"Watch yourself, Caroline," Dad said, his voice now dark too. "Don't push too hard or I'll walk out that door and never come back."

"Do you want me to open it for you, Matthew?"

The silence seemed to last forever. Finally Dad's voice burst out like gunshots. "You want it, Caroline; you got it. I'm gone. I'm out of here."

"Fine. You can leave in the morning."

"The hell with that. I'll leave right now." He paused. "There is a place where I'll be welcome, you know."

"Yes, I'm quite aware of that."

For a few minutes we heard his heavy footsteps moving from the living room to the bathroom to the bedroom. At last we heard the front door open and then slam close. Mom walked around a little after that, as if she was cleaning up or something. Then we heard her crying.

"Do you think we should go down?" Scott whispered.

"What would we say?"

He thought for a second. "I don't know."

She cried for what seemed like hours, but was probably only a few minutes. Then the living room light went off. Immediately we sneaked back to our own rooms.

At breakfast Mom was businesslike. "I'm not going to lie to you. There's been too much fighting around here. You know it and I know it and your dad knows it. It's not good for you and it's not good for us. So today I'm going to see a lawyer about a divorce. It won't be easy. There will be less money, and we'll all have to make sacrifices. But it has to be done." She looked at Scott, then at me. That's when I noticed how red-rimmed her eyes were, and how sad. "This isn't your fault. And it doesn't mean you won't see your dad anymore, or that he doesn't love you. He's your dad, and there's no one in the world who will ever love you like your dad."

Part
Two

Part
Two

Chapter 1

I'd always been a decent student, B's mostly, with a few A's sprinkled in like three-point baskets in a game. But I didn't do so well during my first months at Bothell High. I'd try to pay attention, only my mind would drift in and out. I was good about writing down the homework assignments at the end of classes, but when I got home I'd shoot hoops until dinner, and then I'd shoot some more after dinner.

Eventually Mom would call me in and tell me to get busy on my homework. I'd open a book and start. But then I'd hear her on the phone with her lawyer or her sister or her nursing supervisor, talking about IRA accounts or how my dad had treated her or the possibility of getting more hours at work. And on the nights she wasn't on the phone, I'd find myself listening to the traffic on the streets. Every truck would sound like my dad's truck, coming back home. Only they all drove by, every single one of them, as the minutes ticked away. Finally I'd look up at the clock and it would be ten, too late to get started. So I'd shove my books into my backpack and head off to school the next morning with nothing done.

It was crazy. Basketball tryouts were coming up, and my chances of making the varsity were good. So I should have been working harder than ever. A million times I told myself that starting *now* I'd get to work. But when the weekly grade reports were posted, the name "Nick Abbott" was at the bottom, right down there with "Trent Dawson."

That put me in pretty sad company. Not that Trent was stupid. Every once in a while he'd shock everyone by raising his hand and saying something decent, but most of the time he did nothing and said nothing. The only class he cared about was P.E. Since he never played on school or rec league teams, gym was the only place where he could show his stuff. He treated every run-of-the-mill gym game as if it were some national championship.

That's why what I did was so idiotic. We were playing touch football; I was on defense, free safety. Their quarterback hit Trent with a little check-off pass in the right flat. Trent cut back, raced past a couple of guys, and suddenly he was running in the clear down the sideline.

The guy is fast, the only one in the class who can keep up with me, so it looked like a cinch touchdown. But I had an angle on him, and I had energy to burn, so I chased him down. I caught him about ten yards from the end zone. Instead of tagging him lightly, I gave him a hard push. The instant I did it, I wished I hadn't. Trent was running so fast that my push caused him to lose his balance. He ran flat-footed, his strides too long, for about ten yards. Then he fell, rolling head-over-heels into the drainage ditch between the field and the sidewalk. There's muddy water and green muck in there, and when Trent climbed out of that ditch, slop was oozing off him.

Everybody started laughing... everybody but Trent and me. He stood stock-still for a moment, his mouth tight. Then he charged me, fists flying. I covered up, but he hit me a couple of times in the stomach and once on the side of the head before the teacher, Mr. Shelly, could get him off me. Even with Shelly pulling him away Trent kept swinging. "I'm going to get you, Abbott," he raged. "I'm going to get you."

Shelly spun him around. "You're not going to get anybody, Dawson! Not unless you have a burning desire to spend a month of Saturdays pulling weeds around here. You understand?"

Trent glowered at him, and then at me, his eyes glittering. I'd never seen him like that, but there were stories floating around, stories about what his brother Zack had done to Ross Paulson and Mike Anderson, and how the police had wanted to press criminal charges, especially over Ross, but how Ross's parents were afraid to. If Zack could go crazy, then so could Trent. I didn't want him coming after me. I stuck my hand out. "I'm sorry."

"There," Mr. Shelly said, looking at Trent. "He's apologized. Shake his hand and forget it."

Trent's hand flashed out and slapped mine away. The bell rang and he stormed off the field. After Mr. Shelly watched him go, he turned to me. "Anything happens, anything at all, you tell me."

I didn't see Trent again until last period, geometry with Mrs. Glandon. I'd hoped he'd forgotten about what had happened, but the second my eye caught his, I knew he hadn't.

When geometry ended, I gathered my books and headed for the door. I wanted to get out of school on time, to walk home with the first wave of kids. But as I reached the door, I heard Mrs. Glandon's voice. "Nick Abbott, I want you to stay a minute." She waited until the room was empty, and then she lit into me. "You're failing, Nick. And you don't have much time before the midterm report goes home. I had your brother, so I know your mom and dad, and I know they won't be happy about these grades. It's time to get on the ball."

"Yes, Mrs. Glandon," I said, but she wouldn't let me go until I'd written down all my missing assignments and promised to complete them within a week.

When I finally escaped her room, the buses had left, and the only kids remaining on campus were involved with some activity or other. As I stepped out onto 88th, I could feel the threat all around me, feel it in the silence of the street and the dampness of the air.

At the cul-de-sac before my own block I saw him—and Zack. The two of them were leaning against the mailbox, staring across the street, acting as if they didn't notice me. My heart started pounding and a lump came to my throat. I wanted to turn and run away, the way zebras run away from lions on those TV shows on PBS. But where? And if I did run, what good would it do?

I continued walking, trying hard not to show any fear. When I was about ten feet away, they turned toward me. I nodded as if we were all friends. They nodded back. I walked steadily forward, came even with them, and then past them. A step, another step. They weren't after me. They just happened to be standing there. I'd imagined the whole thing.

I was about to exhale when I heard their footsteps. They were on me before I could turn myself fully around. I toppled over, grabbing at them as they pushed me off the sidewalk and down into the drainage ditch.

Within seconds we were all in the muck, only this time I was at the bottom. Trent or Zack or both of them together were pushing my head down under the water. Before I could breathe, my nose and mouth filled with slime. I fought my way up, gulped air, and then my head was pushed down under. I tried twisting and turning, but they were too strong for me. They kept pushing me down, down, down. I fought, I kicked, I slammed my fists into the mud and water. It was no use. I was drowning. They were killing me.

My eyes rolled inward and a last wave of something close to pleasure filled me. Then, just before I lost consciousness entirely, the hands released me. I felt my head slowly rise out of the water. I was able to breathe air, pure delicious air, and it tasted better than anything I've ever tasted in my entire life. I rolled out of the ditch and lay on my side sucking it in by the gallon.

I heard voices, but I couldn't follow what was being said. Every bit of me concentrated on breathing. Finally I felt a hand under my armpits pulling me to my feet. I stood, shaky in the legs and only half-clear in my mind.

Luke Jackson was helping me up. I knew him a little from

P.E. and from seeing him around in the summer. He lived in the Highlands, the fanciest housing development in the area. A black guy, maybe six four or six five, with a shaved head and one gold earring, new to the neighborhood. We'd been on the same team in gym a couple of times, though we'd never really talked. "You okay?" he asked.

I nodded.

He looked up the street toward where Trent and Zack were walking rapidly away. "Those guys got a little carried away, I'd say." He paused. "You make it home?"

"Yeah," I said, my voice sounding strange. "I can make it home."

He nodded. "All right then. See you tomorrow." He looked down at his muddy pants and shoes. "Damn. They got my clothes all dirty." Then he crossed 104th and headed up his own block. I never even thanked him.

When I opened the front door that afternoon, Scott was on the sofa with his arms wrapped around Katya Ushakov. Their faces both flushed red when they heard me come in, and they jumped apart. But once Katya got a good look at me, she sprang to her feet. "What happened, Nick? Are you all right?"

She walked me straight to the bathroom, Scott trailing behind. She ran the bath and started peeling my clothes off. I was so dazed I didn't object. When I was down to my underwear she scooped up my jeans and sweatshirt. "Where's your washing machine?" she asked Scott.

"I'll show you," he answered.

Once they were gone, I finished undressing and slid into

the tub. I closed my eyes, lay back, and soaked. If I could have, I would have opened my skin and let it warm my insides. Twice I fell asleep, but both times I woke with a start, shaking and gulping air, as if I were somehow back in that ditch, my head underwater. As the water cooled, I drained some off and added more hot. I did that until I'd used every drop. Then I wrapped myself in a towel and went to my room.

I would have liked to have stretched out on my bed and gone to sleep. But I knew Katya and Scott were waiting for an explanation, so I forced myself to go to the front room. She was sitting in the big chair by the window. He had his feet up on the coffee table.

I'd thought about telling them that I'd slipped and fallen head-first into a ditch. But once I saw Katya's face, I couldn't lie. So I told them what happened. "Anyway, it's over with now," I said.

Katya's eyes widened. "What do you mean, it's over with? You've got to call the police. They could have killed you."

"Calling the police would make it worse."

"How?" she demanded. "How could it make it worse?"

"Nothing would happen to them, Katya. And then they'd beat me up again."

Her face reddened in anger. "So you're going to let them get away with it? They try to kill you, and you do nothing?"

Scott came to my defense. "Nick's right, Katya. The Dawsons are trouble. You don't want them after you."

She wheeled on him. "And what about the next boy? What if they actually kill the next boy?"

"Katya," Scott said, trying to soothe her. "Nobody is going to get killed."

Katya pointed her finger at me. "*He* almost got killed! Didn't you hear him! Your own brother! What if this Luke hadn't been there? What then?"

She stared at Scott, stared at him the way a scientist looks at some strange bacteria under a microscope. Then, before Scott answered, she grabbed her clarinet case and stormed out of our house.

Scott started toward the door, stopped, then turned on me. "Thanks a lot, Nick."

"What did I do?" I asked, but he just walked past me and went downstairs.

Dad phoned that night. I was upstairs reading when Mom called up to me. "Hey, Nick," he said when I took the receiver from her. "How are you, Son?"

Hearing his voice made me feel better. I still wasn't used to his being gone, and whenever he didn't call for a while, I started worrying. I knew guys who hadn't seen their dads in years.

He asked how I was doing in school and what my teachers were like. "Look," he said at last, "the Sonics have an intrasquad game Friday night. I've got courtside seats. What do you say? Do you want to go?"

"Yeah," I said instantly. "It sounds terrific."

"Great," he answered, and I could feel the relief in his voice. "Listen. I already talked to your brother, and he's busy, so I've got an extra ticket. If you've got a buddy you'd like to bring along, go ahead and ask him." He paused. "Or her. You got a girl you'd like to bring along?"

I felt myself go red in the face. "No, Dad."

He laughed. "All right. Well, put your mom on now. We've got to work out the details."

After I handed the receiver to Mom, I went downstairs to the den where Scott was watching a Simpson's rerun on the tube—one about the Kwik-E-Mart. We'd laughed a lot the first time we'd seen it, but that evening—while we heard the murmur of Mom's voice on the phone upstairs—neither of us laughed once.

On the telephone Dad's voice had been off somehow, cheerful on top but sad underneath. That's how I felt, too. I'd thought that what I'd wanted more than anything was for Dad to look at me, look hard and long at what I could do, not just glance at me for a second or two before turning back to Scott. I had a feeling that was going to happen now. I was going to get exactly what I'd always wanted.

But I would have given that up if I could have had him living at home again, the way he used to, only without the fighting. I'd have gone back to being the second son for that.

Chapter 2 At school the next day I kept expecting Trent to be around every corner. I don't know what more I thought he was going to do. I didn't really expect him to choke me to death in the hallway in front of a thousand kids. Still, I didn't think he'd tell me how sorry he was and invite me to his birthday party, either.

I didn't see him until P.E. In the locker room he ignored me as we suited up. No threat about how I'd better be watching out, how he was going to finish me off some day. Nothing at all. I breathed a little easier, vowing to myself never to cross swords with him again. He could score all the touchdowns he wanted.

The guy who did talk to me was Luke Jackson, but it wasn't about Zack or Trent or what had happened. As we ran our warm-up laps together, we talked hoops. All through that P.E. class, I thought about my dad's extra ticket and how I owed Luke. At the end of class I asked him if he wanted to go. The answer was immediate. "Sure do. If I'm going to live here I've got to start rooting for the Sonics."

After school on Friday we walked to my house together. When he saw my court, he licked his lips. "How about a little one-on-one while we wait for your dad?"

We played all afternoon. I'd known from gym class that he was good, but now I saw just how good. He was quick, with soft hands and the touch of a natural scorer. He had the attitude of a scorer too. When his shots were dropping, he rebounded and played tough defense. But when he hit a cold spell, his whole game fell apart. He stopped blocking out on rebounds; he stopped hustling after loose balls.

Our games had a crazy rhythm to them. He'd jump out way ahead or he'd fall way behind. Whichever it was, I'd play my steady game, hoping either to catch him when he cooled down or to hold him off when his hot streak came. Sometimes I did; sometimes I didn't.

We'd played a half dozen games before Dad's truck pulled into the driveway. Then the three of us shot around for a little while. In the beginning Dad was unimpressed. Then Luke caught fire and sank about a dozen shots in a row, opening Dad's eyes. "You going out for the Bothell team?" he asked.

"You bet," Luke answered.

My father smiled. "I'll tell you what. I'm jealous of your coach, because I'm looking at two parts of a pretty good-looking team."

Dad and I went inside to tell Mom we were off. Scott was in our downstairs den watching television. I saw Dad look that way, but Scott didn't even come up to say hello. Mom stood in the doorway, her hands on her hips. "I'll have Nick back by eleven at the latest," Dad said.

Mom looked right past him to me. "Have fun."

"I will," I managed.

Things got better once we piled into the truck. The scrimmage was at Seattle Pacific University. We stopped at Kidd Valley for hamburgers, fries, and milk shakes, then hopped on the freeway at 145th for the ride into Seattle. We talked basketball all the way down to the game — pro hoops, college hoops, high school hoops. Luke knew as much about the players and teams as Dad and I did, which made it easy.

You hear you've got courtside seats, and you figure that the seats are really three, or five, or ten rows up. But we sat on folding chairs at mid-court. The Sonics were right there, and I mean, *right there.*

At the airport I'd once seen the Seattle Mariners. They weren't all that different from other men in the airport. A little bigger maybe, with a little less fat around the gut, and a lot more jewelry around their necks. If I hadn't spotted Ken Griffey Jr., I might not have recognized any of them.

Being close to the Sonics was entirely different. There was no way I wouldn't have recognized them as basketball players. It wasn't just their height, though they were incredibly tall. It was more the muscles. The power forwards, the centers — those guys were absolutely massive. During warm-ups I stared at them, my mouth hanging open. Dad nudged me. "Forget about those big guys, Nick. You can't learn anything from them. Keep your eyes on Gary Payton."

When I was little, Michael Jordan was the player I'd dreamed of being. Me and every other kid in the country. In my closet I had Jordan shoes and a Jordan jersey. But Jordan was *too* good. I've got some of his games on video. Every once in a while I watch one, hoping to pick up some moves. And sometimes I do, but always from one of his teammates. The things Jordan did — it's as if he was from some other planet. You can't even pretend you can be like him.

Gary Payton has to work to be great. When I watch him, I can visualize myself doing the things he does. Sometimes I'll even stop the cassette and practice one of his moves in the mirror, and then try it out the next time I play.

The Sonics were playing an intrasquad game, not even an exhibition, the Green against the Orange. Half of the players I'd never heard of. "Who are these guys?" Luke asked in a whisper as they warmed up. We were so close he was afraid one of them might hear.

My father leaned toward him. "They're from everywhere. High schools, junior colleges, South America, Lithuania. There are ten guys fighting for one or two spots on the roster. The ones that don't make it will end up in the CBA or in Europe— or back home shooting around at the rec center." My father looked out to the court. "They'll play hard. This is the chance of a lifetime for them."

He was right. Once the game started, it was the no-namers who were flying up and down the court, hurling themselves on every loose ball, crashing the boards. Payton and the other veterans went at a slower pace. The season was weeks away, and they were just loosening up. Sometimes they almost seemed amused by the fury around them.

There was one guard from Tennessee who was really playing super. He wasn't passing the ball much—none of the no-namers were doing much passing—but when he had the ball he made slashing drives to the hole or else pulled up for high arching rainbows from outside the three-point line. If you didn't know better, you'd have thought he was the all-star point guard and that Payton was the nobody hoping to catch on with the team.

Early in the third quarter the Tennessee guy stole the ball on a double-team. He came out of the traffic like a bullet, heading upcourt ahead of the pack.

Or almost ahead of the pack. Payton was the last defender. I figured the Tennessee guy would pull up for a jumper, and that must have been what Payton thought too. Instead, he gave Payton a stutter step, then blew by him and soared for an amazing tomahawk jam. Like the other two thousand or so in the stands, I jumped to my feet and let out a roar.

When we settled back into our seats, Dad leaned over to me. "Mark my words. Payton will make him pay."

All through the third quarter and into the fourth, Payton was almost invisible. He made some nice passes, played some good defense, but you didn't notice him. Then, with about three minutes left and his team down six points, he turned his game up a notch. First he hit a three-pointer, then stole the ball and drove for a thundering jam of his own.

The Tennessee kid suddenly looked rattled. He took an off-balance jumper that missed badly, and Payton brought the ball down with a chance to steal a win.

The seconds were ticking away...13...12...11. A couple of guys flashed into the key, but still Payton kept his dribble up top, his eyes locked on the Tennessee kid: 6...5...4. Then Payton made his move. A hard drive to his right, and a lightning-quick crossover dribble that left the Tennessee guy flailing. Payton took the ball hard to the glass, and his scoop lay-in dropped through just as the horn sounded. Everyone was up and cheering, and Payton grinned ear-to-ear right in the face of the Tennessee guy.

After the game we went to Starbucks for muffins and hot chocolate. We sat talking about the game, always coming back to Payton's winning shot. "Talk about knowing how much time is left," Luke said. "Man, he cut that close!"

We finished eating. Dad dropped Luke off and drove me

home. When he pulled into the driveway, he turned in his seat to face me. "You saw how Payton played tonight," he said, "how he took the game into his own hands at the end. That's how I want you to play. Pass all you want throughout the whole game, lead the world in assists, make your coach and teammates happy. But when it's crunch time, when the game is on the line, you take the final shot. You understand what I'm saying. You take it."

"I understand, Dad."

He reached over, roughed up my hair. "Good." Then he looked at me. "I miss you, Nick."

That lump came back to my throat. "I miss you too," I said.

He reached across me and opened my door. "You better get inside. We're late, and I don't want your mom to worry."

Chapter 3 Monday at P.E., Mr. Shelly announced that for the next few weeks we'd be playing a basketball tournament. Then he named me as one of the six captains. That pumped me up, because it meant he knew that I'd been a player in junior high. And if he knew about me, then Coach O'Leary, the varsity head coach, knew about me too.

We used the beauty-contest method for picking teams. I picked Luke first. After that I got Leo Devencenzi and Casey Russell, both of whom were okay players and old Canyon Park buddies. The last guy was somebody whose name I didn't know, an uncoordinated kid who had some size.

Shelly went over the rules for the tournament. Basic stuff:

Call your own fouls. Captains settle arguments. Then, right before the games started, Coach O'Leary came out of the coaches' office and took a seat on a folding chair under the scoreboard.

O'Leary was huge, six six and probably close to three hundred pounds of muscle and fat. He had thinning red hair and a freckled face and arms. His voice went with his body, a booming voice that filled whatever room he was in and the one next to it. I once watched him order a sandwich at Safeway. "Ahh, put a couple more slices on there, buddy, will you?" O'Leary thundered. The deli man, laughing, obliged with about another half pound of salami.

This was my chance to show O'Leary exactly what I could do. Then came the kick in the face. The team we were playing had Trent Dawson on it.

As soon as Dawson saw the match-up he pointed to me. "I'll take Nick Abbott." I figured he'd really take me, fouling me hard and often. My heart raced. What could I do? If I let him run over me, he'd make me look like a clown in front of O'Leary. But if I called him for fouling me, I'd run the risk of having him come after me again, and I didn't want that.

The amazing thing is, I never had to decide. Not that Trent didn't play hard, because he did. He had a deceptive stutter-step dribble, was fast on his feet and with his hands, and dived after every loose ball as if it were a million dollar bill. When I challenged him by driving to the basket, he made me pay with hard fouls, but I did the same to him. What he didn't do was give me the elbow in the gut or the forearm to the chest that were his trademarks.

With under a minute left we were down by one. The whole game I'd been feeding Luke, and he'd been filling the hoop. But I remembered what my dad had said about crunch time, and I took the game into my hands.

I was dribbling at the top of the key, keeping the ball out of Trent's reach. With my eyes I showed Luke where I wanted the screen. He set it, on Trent's right. Trent felt him there and anticipated my move in that direction. So I faked that way and went the other way. Trent got his feet tangled, and I was in the clear for a pull-up jumper from just outside the free-throw line. No doubt about it. Swish! Right in the heart!

Shelly, standing in center of the huge gym, blew his whistle. "That's it, gentlemen. Shower up!"

As I headed to the locker room, Coach O'Leary crossed over to me. "You're Scott Abbott's brother, right?"

"Yeah. I'm Nick Abbott."

"Well, that was nice clutch shooting at the end there, Nick. Real nice."

"Thanks, Coach," I answered, trying not to smile. "Thanks a lot."

After school Luke came over to shoot around. He was as pumped as I was. "I wonder how many of my pretty jumpers O'Leary saw fall through the net?"

"Quite a few, because of all those pretty assists I fed you."

He laughed. "You don't get an assist unless I make the shot. Remember that, Mr. Point Guard. You need me."

We shot around a little, and then I asked him if he wanted to go one-on-one. He shook his head. "No more of that for a while."

"Why not?"

"You know what this so-called basketball tournament really is? It's a tryout, that's what it is. That's why O'Leary was there today, why he's going to be there every day. The guy will be watching every gym class, picking out his team. So we'd better work on some two-man games, screen and rolls, lob passes over the top, that sort of stuff. We caught his eye today. Now we've got to make sure we keep it."

For the next hour we worked at getting in sync. When you play point guard, it's not enough to hit a guy with a pass, you've got to hit him so that he's in rhythm, so that he can dribble or shoot without a moment's hesitation, without the slightest fumbling for the ball. To do that, you've got to know exactly where he wants the ball and exactly when he wants it. And you've got to have the right amount of zip on the ball, too. You can't be knocking the guy down, or making him wait. The timing has to be perfect, and perfect takes practice.

After an hour of lob passes and skip passes off imaginary pick and rolls, we needed a break. I went inside and brought out a liter of Pepsi. We sat on the back steps and passed the bottle back and forth. The Pepsi was cold and sweet going down.

"That Dawson is a pretty good ballplayer," Luke said.

I took a long swig. "Yeah, he's tough."

"He's the only guy out there besides you and me who has a chance to make the varsity."

I laughed. "Trent Dawson? He won't turn out for the team. No way."

Luke took the Pepsi from me. "He played pretty hard for someone who's not interested."

My mother's car pulled up. She smiled and waved hello, then went inside. Luke and I were just getting ready to shoot again when the back door popped open. "I'm sorry, Luke, you're going to have go home now. I need to talk to Nick."

Luke's eyebrows raised. He could hear the anger in Mom's voice, see it in her face. "Tomorrow, Nick," he said.

I'd barely made it inside when Mom started waving a piece of paper in front of my nose. "What is this, young man? What is this?"

"I don't know," I answered. "I can't even see it."

She thrust the paper into my face. "All right. See it."

Bothell High sends home midterm grades. They don't really count for anything; they're sort of a preview of coming attractions. What was coming for me was a horror film.

"Four D's," she fumed, her eyes wide with shock. "Four! And in all your important classes. English, history, science, math."

"I'll start studying," I mumbled. "Don't worry."

"You bet you'll start, young man. From now on, when my car pulls into the driveway, Luke goes home and you go upstairs and hit the books."

"But Mom..."

"No buts. You're lucky I'm letting you shoot around at all. If you spent a quarter of the time and energy on schoolwork that you do on basketball, you'd have straight A's."

Chapter 4

I stomped up to my room, but when I cooled off I had to admit she was right. I did have to bring my grades up to C's or I wouldn't be playing on any team— varsity or junior varsity. When I broke the news to Luke the next day, he shrugged, saying, "Won't matter. In two weeks daylight-saving time ends. It'll be too dark to shoot hoops much past five anyway."

The good thing was that our P.E. games kept going great. We were winning almost all of them, right under the eye of Coach O'Leary. The only team that gave us a battle was Trent's. And it really wasn't his team; it was him. It was hard to get in a flow when Trent was guarding me. Sometimes I'd be so worn down by his constant pressure that I'd get rid of the ball too soon, putting Devencenzi in the role of play-maker, a role he couldn't handle. Other times I'd get caught up in the one-on-one challenge and try to do too much on my own. That frustrated Luke. He'd clap his hands together, meaning: *Get me the ball! Get me the ball!*

Saturday morning Dad called. Mom had made me promise I'd study that morning, but when he said he wanted to spend the day with Scott and me, she relented. "No television tonight though," she said.

I waited for Dad in the front room. Not Scott, though. He stayed downstairs in the den with Mom. While I checked over the sports page, I could hear the two of them arguing.

The pick-up pulled into the driveway. The truck door opened and slammed shut. I opened the front door as Dad, smiling ear-to-ear, came up the porch steps and into the house. "Hey,

Nick," he said, first shaking my hand and then pulling me to him. "What's up?"

"Not much," I answered. He let go of me, and we stood looking at each other as Scott, with my mother behind him, came up the stairs and into the room. My father nodded to him, smiled. But there was no hug, no handshake even. "How are you, Son?" he asked, his voice formal.

"I'm doing fine," Scott replied. "How about you?"

"Can't complain. Can't complain." The four of us stood awkwardly until Dad spoke again. "I've got nothing big planned. I thought we'd just hang out together, the three of us. Maybe shoot some hoops in the back yard, then bike the Burke-Gilman. What do you say?"

"I can't," Scott answered. "Katya's coming over."

"You think maybe you could cancel that?" Dad asked.

Scott shook his head. "We need to work on some songs."

For a moment Dad was silent. Then a false cheeriness came to his voice and face. "Well, if you can't, you can't." He turned to me. "How about you, Nick? Does that sound like a plan?"

"You bet," and now it was my voice that was too happy.

"All right then, let's go shoot around. I bought a new ball."

Mom spoke. "I'm going to be out most of the day, Nick. So take your key in case no one is here when you get back."

"Okay," I said, realizing for the first time that Dad no longer had a key to our house, and never would have one again.

Dad's new basketball was one of those outdoor balls that feel like leather but hold up on asphalt. It felt nice in my hand, and I was stroking the jumper from everywhere. Dad was praising me too, telling me how good my game looked. Even when I told him about my grades, he only shrugged. "You'll pull those up. You're a smart kid."

It should have been fun, and it would have been, only we could hear Scott, and then Scott and Katya, practicing. I don't know the name of the song they were playing. Something by Miles Davis probably, because Scott was always talking about Miles Davis. Whatever it was, it was about the saddest song in the world. Sometimes I'd say something and Dad wouldn't answer at all.

We'd been playing about an hour when Steve Clay appeared at the back gate. My father invited him into the back yard. "It's holding up great," Dad declared, his eyes scanning the court. "No cracks, the support straight as an arrow."

"It does look good," Steve Clay answered, proud of the work he'd done.

I took a shot, missed, and the ball bounded to him. He caught it, but instead of shooting or passing, he held it. "Listen, if I can get Trent to come over, would you be interested in a little two-on-two?"

"Sure," Dad answered eagerly, without even asking me.

Steve Clay smiled broadly. "Great. I'll go get him."

As soon as he left the yard, I turned on Dad. "What did you do that for? I don't want Trent around here."

He shrugged. "Why not? It'll be fun."

"I'm sick of Trent Dawson. I have to play against him in P.E. all the time."

"Stop complaining, Nick. We'll kick their butts, and that'll make you feel better."

I didn't say anything more, but inside I was seething. All I'd wanted was to spend one day with Dad. Just one day. And instead I was going to spend a good part of it with Trent Dawson.

Then, the unexpected — Steve Clay returned without Trent. He leaned over the gate and called to us. "Trent's gone off somewhere with Zack. Sorry."

Dad nodded. "Some other time, then."

It was lunchtime, so we loaded my bike into the back of the truck and drove to the Ranch Drive-in, where we had burgers and fries. Then we biked all the way to Matthew's Beach on the Burke-Gilman trail. On the way back we saw Trent on the railroad trestle with Zack and Zack's friends. They were smoking cigarettes, drinking beer, and throwing rocks at the ducks swimming in the slough.

Chapter 5 Things settled into a routine. Every day after school I'd shoot around with Luke until Mom drove up. As soon as she pulled on the emergency brake, Luke would grab his sweatshirt, give me a wave goodbye, and I'd go upstairs to my room to study. About an hour later Mom would call Scott and me down for dinner, and afterwards it was back to the books.

Every time a teacher posted scores, my percentage went up. Unless I totally bombed the finals, I was likely to end up with C+'s and B's. Nothing that would please my mom, but plenty good to keep me eligible. The Sunday night before tryouts officially began, Luke phoned. "Your grades a problem?"

"No," I said. "Not anymore. How about yours?"

"I told you, Nick. Nothing but A's for me. Always and forever."

Neither of us spoke for a moment. Then I said what we were both thinking. "You think we can make the varsity?"

Luke laughed. "No way we're playing JV's. We're going to make the varsity and we're going to play serious minutes."

I had trouble sleeping that night. You see other guy's games, guys like Matt Markey or even my brother. You watch them play and you can spot weaknesses right away. But you can't see your own game, or at least not clearly. You never know what you look like to a coach.

Monday dragged. I couldn't pay attention in class, and my stomach was rolling over. I started worrying that I was coming down with diarrhea. I could imagine myself during tryouts racing to the toilet every five minutes.

Classes finally ended and I headed to the gym. I walked slowly, trying not to seem too eager. On the way I checked out the other guys heading to the gym. Some of them were returning starters like Carlos Fabroa and Tom McShane, who'd played center and power forward. But there were lots of guys I didn't know.

I swung open the locker room door and stepped inside. Immediately I spotted Luke. From the way he'd talked on the telephone and acted at P.E., I thought he'd be completely cool. But I could see he was as nervous as I was. His brown skin looked less brown, and his eyes darted around. "Hey, Luke," I croaked, but he barely nodded back to me.

I understood. My mouth was too dry for me to do much talking either. I opened a locker, yanked off my pants and shirt, and pulled on my gym clothes. I was about to close up the locker when I got the shock of my life. In walked Trent Dawson.

What he was doing there was a total mystery. Okay, so he played tough defense and could create his own shot off that stutter-step dribble of his. But the guy had none of the other stuff you need to succeed. He never stuck with anything; he didn't know how to follow rules or play as a member of a team; he was flunking all his classes. For him to think he could make the varsity was a total joke. Only it wasn't funny, because I had a sinking feeling that somehow, some way, he'd mess things up for me.

I wasn't the only guy stunned to see Dawson suiting up. The whole locker room hushed as he entered. I guess he could feel all the eyes on him, because without warning he turned on Brian Chang, a junior guard. "What are you staring at?" he snarled. Chang looked away quickly.

When I stepped on the court, all I heard was the sound of basketballs bouncing and shoes squeaking on the hardwood floor. It seemed as though there were one hundred guys trying out, though the real number was closer to thirty.

I stayed away from the court where Carver, Fabroa, and the other varsity players were shooting, instead choosing a basket off to the side where Luke was warming up. When he spotted me, he fed me a bounce pass. I took the ball in for a lay-in. Just seeing one shot go down made me feel better. After that it was jumpers, runners in the key, a few free throws.

Eventually Coach O'Leary blew his whistle and called us together. "Good to see you out here!" he boomed. His big face was bright red and little beads of sweat had formed on his forehead. He held a basketball in front of him, and he swatted it hard with his open palm. He smiled. "Now I know what you're thinking, especially you new guys. That I'm a fat, freckled Irishman with a beer belly. And it's all true. But I know this game, gentlemen. I know this game. And if you listen to me, I'll teach it to you." He bounced the ball. "Three lines, everybody, pass and cut, pass and cut. Let's see if you know how to run a fast break."

In a game you want to be the one to finish off a fast break, to rack up the easy two points and improve your shooting stats. But that first time through the line, guys would pass and pass until we were on top of the hoop and finally somebody had to shoot. Everybody was competing to seem the least selfish player—everybody except Trent.

His first time down he took a pass at half court and then dribbled all the way in for the lay-in, leaving his teammates totally out of it. It was comical, and I saw a grin crease O'Leary's face. I don't think he'd ever seen that done before. He blew his whistle, explained the point of the drill to Trent, and play resumed.

Next came a rebounding drill, keeping the ball alive off the glass. Eight lines, four guys per group—nothing fancy. O'Leary was looking for some legs that could elevate. It was a chance for Luke to show his athleticism, and he did.

After that it was chest passes and bounce passes, the boring stuff. While we were doing those drills, O'Leary came around and took down our height, weight, and the position we were trying out for. "Point guard," I said, when he came to me.

"So you want to run the whole show?"

"No," I said quickly. His red eyebrows went up quizzically. "I mean yes." The eyebrows went higher. "I mean no."

He laughed. "Relax, Nick. I'm just having a little fun." He started to walk away, then turned back. "Your brother isn't turning out?"

I shook my head. "He's playing his trumpet instead."

Coach O'Leary nodded. "That's what I'd heard. Is he any good?"

"I don't know much about music," I said, "but he sounds good to me."

"Well, we're going to miss him. He was a good guy to have on the team. Kept other guys steady, always gave his best. You tell him I said that."

"I will," I replied, thinking how surprised my father would have been to have heard O'Leary praise Scott.

A couple minutes later O'Leary blew his whistle and called us to him. "There are thirty of you out here, but there are only twelve uniforms in my office. To make this team, you've got five days to prove to me you want a uniform more than the guy standing next to you." He motioned to the other side of the court. "Over there is Darren Nolan, our team manager. If you want to stay on this team, you treat him with respect. Those little pieces of paper he's sticking on the wall are your squad assignments. Find your name and pick up the right color jersey." He stopped, and a little smile came to his eyes. "Okay, gentlemen, time to show what you've got."

59

It was chaos then. Guys crowded around the slips of white paper stuck up on the wall underneath the farthest hoop. It took me a while, but finally I found my name. I was on the Red team. I scanned the list of names. A rush of adrenaline came when I saw Luke was on my team, but it disappeared when I saw Trent was on the Red team, too.

I couldn't believe my bad luck, then realized it hadn't been luck at all. O'Leary wanted us comfortable on the court, so he'd teamed us with guys from our P.E. class. It cut down on the time it would take to get used to teammates. For most guys the set-up probably worked. For most guys.

I was the point guard, our team's main ball handler. Only I couldn't get going. My hands didn't feel as if they were mine. The ball kept getting away from me, off my knee, my toe, my thigh, as if it had a will of its own.

Luke was feeling the pressure too. When he was wide open, he short-armed his shots, barely hitting the rim. When he was closely guarded, he flung up wild shots instead of passing off. Part of his trouble was my fault. I wasn't getting the ball to him in rhythm.

Afterwards Luke and I walked home together. Most of the way we didn't talk; we were both too down. But just before he peeled off, Luke motioned toward Trent, who was a block ahead. "He's probably got a better chance of making the team than I do. He rebounds well, chases down everything, never quits."

I scoffed at that. "Come on. The guy's a wrestler, not a basketball player. He'd foul out of a real game in about three minutes."

Luke snorted. "Yeah, well, better to be a wrestler than to be nothing, which was what I was." We lapsed into silence. Then Luke forced himself to smile. "It was only one day. We've got four more."

"Right," I answered, trying to pump myself up, "we'll show them tomorrow."

Chapter 6 At dinner, Scott was full of talk about his jazz band. They were going to Port Townsend for some competition, and if they did well they'd end up in Monterey, California, over Christmas. "The school will pay for the hotel," he said, "but I have to come up with airfare."

"Don't worry," Mom reassured him. "We'll find the money. And if you make it to California, I'm going with you."

After dinner I was brooding upstairs about my own future when I heard a knock at the front door. I thought it might be Dad, coming to check on how tryouts had gone, so I hustled downstairs to get the door. But when I opened up Steve Clay was on the porch.

"Can I talk to your mom?" he asked.

"Sure," I said, then I half-closed the door, leaving him out on the porch in the dark. Mom was downstairs working on the computer. "I wonder what he wants," she said as she stood up.

Back upstairs, she opened the door wide and invited him in. I went to the kitchen where I could hear, but wouldn't have to say anything. Steve Clay wouldn't sit down until my mom asked him three times. Even then he wouldn't take anything, not coffee, not a Pepsi, not even water. Upstairs in his room Scott hit a high note on the trumpet and held it for what seemed like forever. From where I sat I could see Steve Clay smile. "He's good."

"Yes, he is," my mother answered, pleased.

He coughed. "Listen, what I'm about to ask is pretty strange, and I won't be angry if you say no. In fact I'm expecting you to say no." He stopped.

"Go on," my mother said.

I leaned forward to listen.

"Well, for the last few months Trent has shown an interest in basketball." He motioned toward me and I quickly looked away. "That's probably because of Nick. Trent wouldn't admit it, but he admires Nick, especially the way Nick can control the whole basketball court, run things." He laughed, a dry laugh. "Maybe that's because Trent can't control much of anything. But I feel if he could make the varsity, it might turn him around. He might learn some discipline, dedicate himself to something . . ." His voice trailed off.

I didn't know what he was driving at and neither did Mom. "I'm glad Trent is interested in basketball," she said, "and I'm glad he admires my son, but I'm not sure what you're asking."

Steve Clay breathed in deeply, exhaled. "Well, here it is. Last week I got a job with Microsoft. It's just custodial; I don't know anything about computers. But that's not the point. The point is that by the time I get off work, it's late. I've been taking Trent to the junior high to shoot around, but it's pitch black where those courts are. What I'd like to do, if you'd let me, is shoot around with Trent in your back yard when I get home from work. An hour or so is what I was thinking."

I could see the startled look on my mother's face. "We don't have light in our back yard either," she said.

He shrugged. "You've got a floodlight over your garage. And there's the moon. We could see well enough."

I knew how Mom felt about the Dawsons. There was no way she was going to have Trent in our yard. No way at all.

"I admire what you're doing," she said. "Trent has needed someone like you in his life. You're welcome to use our back yard."

My mouth dropped open.

Steve Clay smiled broadly as he made his way to the door. "Thank you. Thank you very much."

After he'd left, I stormed into the front room. "Are you crazy? You're going to let Trent Dawson shoot around in our yard!"

"With Steve Clay, I am. Yes."

"That is so unfair. It's my back yard, my hoop, and you won't let me shoot around after dinner. But Trent Dawson can?"

"You need to study, Nick."

"I need to study? Well, if I need to study, then he needs to live in the library. The guy is flunking everything. And have you thought about all the stuff in our shed? Because he's a thief, you know. He'll steal anything. And what are you going to do if Zack starts—"

"That's enough, Nick." Her mouth was drawn tight and her

voice was cold with fury, but I was plenty angry too.

"What do you mean, 'That's enough'?"

"I mean that I'm aware this is a risk. Okay? But I'm willing to take it. And you're old enough to figure out why. So take yourself up to your room and do it."

She walked past me and back downstairs. I stood, still in shock, for a long moment. Then I climbed upstairs to my own room.

Studying was out of the question. There was nothing on the radio; nothing on the television. I picked up a *Sports Illustrated,* flipped through it, threw it down on the ground.

I decided to call Dad. I wasn't sure what I was going to say, whether I'd tell him about Trent or not. I just wanted to talk to him.

We have a phone upstairs in the hallway between Scott's room and mine. I punched in Dad's number. The phone rang once, twice. But instead of his voice, I heard a woman's. "Hello." Her voice was bright and sunny.

The blood drained out of me. I stood still, holding the receiver tight. "Hellooooo," she repeated, laughing. "Anybody there?"

I hung up without a word.

Chapter 7 The next day my legs felt heavy and my mind dull. But oddly enough, I played better; maybe I was just too tired to be jittery, too brain-dead to care. Whatever the reason, I saw the whole court. And that's what playing point guard comes to—seeing the court. When I'm on, it's as if I'm going at full speed while everyone else is moving in slow motion.

Luke was playing better too. I was getting him the ball where he could do damage, and his outside jumper was dropping. Swish! ... Swish! ... Swish! When the defenders tightened up on him, he cut back door and I hit him with bounce passes for driving lay-ins.

It wasn't as if I purposefully froze Trent out. Luke had the hot hand so I kept feeding him the ball, which is what you're supposed to do. But I'll admit that I could see Trent was getting frustrated; I could see it in his face, see it in the elbows he started tossing around. And I'll also admit I didn't do anything about it.

The explosion came just before the final scrimmage ended. We were playing the Gold team, and we were crushing them. Trent grabbed a defensive rebound and burst out of the pack, dribbling hard down the right side of the court. I took the center lane and Luke was to my left. Trent should have given me the ball, but he probably figured he wouldn't have gotten it back, and he was probably right.

When he reached the key, he did a spin move on the first guy and blew right by him. But Matt Markey was clogging the middle, holding his position. Trent bowled him over— totally flattening him—just as he threw up his shot, an incredible spinning lay-in that tickled the twine as the two of them crashed to the ground. It was the shot of the day, but O'Leary blew the whistle. "That's a charge!" he called out. "No basket."

Trent climbed to his feet. "You suck, old man," he muttered, just loud enough for O'Leary to hear him.

"What did you say?" O'Leary demanded.

Trent glared at him. "I said, 'You suck.' And I'll say it again: 'You suck.'"

Coach O'Leary's face and ears went bright red. "Off the court, Dawson. Off the court right this instant. And don't come back unless you bring a letter of apology and a better attitude. I don't need you, kid; you need me."

Trent pointed his finger at O'Leary. "Let me tell you something, Fatso. I don't need you." Then he looked around at all of us. "I don't need any of you. This whole thing sucks!" He grabbed the basketball from Markey and slammed it down. It bounced at least thirty feet in the air. With that he stormed off the court. A couple of guys laughed nervously. But O'Leary glared at them, and they went quiet.

Practice ended about ten minutes later. In the locker room evidence of Trent's fury was everywhere. The trash cans had all been tipped over and kicked around. Any clothes or shoes that had been left out had been thrown every which way.

"There's one less guy to worry about," Tom McShane said as he righted one of the garbage cans. "And I'll tell you, I'm glad he's gone. I didn't like playing against him. The guy never let you breathe."

"That's the truth," Carlos Fabroa chimed in.

On the walk home I expected Luke to be falling all over himself thanking me. After all, he'd scored about fifty points, and forty-eight had come on assists from me. His chances for making the team had soared, yet he was strangely quiet. "What's eating you?" I asked at last.

"I've been thinking about what Tom and Carlos said."

"That they're glad Trent quit? I guess just about everybody feels that way."

"No, not that."

"What then?"

"About how they said they hated to have Trent guard them."

"Yeah, so?"

"Well, so would every player on every other team, wouldn't they? Dawson plays tough defense, really in your face, non-stop."

"What are you saying?"

"I'm saying I hope Trent does come back tomorrow. We'd be a better team with him than without him."

"You've got to be kidding. The guy thinks only of himself. He has zero commitment to his teammates."

"Come on, Nick. As if you do."

"What's that supposed to mean?"

"It means that we're all the same out there, looking out for ourselves, trying to shine for Coach. Me, you, Trent, everybody."

"All right," I admitted, "that's true enough. At least now, during tryouts. But after tryouts, I'll change and you'll change, but Trent wouldn't."

"You don't know that."

"I do know it."

We walked for a while in silence. I could tell he was angry.

"Look," I said, "I don't know what we're arguing about. You heard O'Leary. He's off the team unless he apologizes, and there's no way in the world he will. So let's just forget about him. Okay?"

"Yeah, sure," Luke answered, but we never did get talking about anything else.

That night at dinner I kept going over the scrimmage in my mind, seeing times when I could have fed Trent a nice pass but hadn't. Just a couple of hoops, and he might not have blown up.

"Something wrong, Nick?" Mom asked.

I shook my head. "Nothing."

Up in my room, I thought about the woman who was living with Dad. I didn't want to meet her or even see her. I couldn't imagine having to live the way Trent did—with different guys in the house all the time. Having different men eat at the table, shower in the bathroom, sit on the sofa in the front room, and then go to bed with my mom—I couldn't take that.

I got so sick of thinking about Trent that I was actually glad when I remembered I had homework to do in geometry. I opened my book and started in.

The problems at the top of the page were easy, but the word problems at the bottom were killers. They were all about picture frames and gardens with borders and rectangular swimming pools with square decks and circular spas.

I'd been working about thirty minutes when the gate leading to my back yard creaked open. That was followed by the steady *thump thump thump* of a basketball being dribbled on concrete. Beneath me, in the darkness, were Steve Clay and Trent.

It's crazy how life is sometimes. A day earlier I'd been angry at the thought of his shooting baskets in my back yard. A few hours earlier I'd been telling Luke that we were better off without him. But now I found myself hoping he would return to the team. If he'd quit entirely on his own, it wouldn't have mattered so much. But I didn't like thinking that my selfishness drove him off the team.

I stood at the window watching them play, watching the way they moved in the milky darkness. Steve Clay was different from my dad, quieter. There was no coaching going on, no teaching at all. Every once in a while he'd say, "Nice shot" or "Good move," and Trent would smile, a crooked little smile I'd never seen before. It was peaceful, watching them, and it must have been peaceful to play that way.

Not that Trent was just throwing stuff up, not caring. That wasn't it at all. He was methodically working on bank shots from ten to fifteen feet out. His jumper was pretty good, too. In the summer he'd shot line drives. Now he was squaring himself up, getting a nice arc, and putting backspin on his shots. And they were going down, one after the other. I wondered where the change had come from, and then a dizzying thought hit me: his shot looked like my shot. He was copying me.

They stayed for an hour. I didn't watch the whole time. Instead I went back to my geometry problems. Hearing the basketball bouncing outside was soothing, and I was able to concentrate and get them done.

Around eleven I went to bed. But instead of sleeping I found myself staring at the ceiling. A rush of loneliness grabbed me and held me, and when it finally let go, another feeling—equally strange, equally unexpected—took its place. I was jealous of Trent Dawson, jealous that he had Steve Clay—who wasn't even his father—shooting hoops with him, watching out for him.

Chapter 8

Trent was back at tryouts the next day. As soon as he took the court, he handed a note to Coach O'Leary. I saw it, a scrawled thing in sloppy handwriting and in pencil. O'Leary looked at it for about one second, then started sputtering. "What language is this? English? Spanish? Chinese? Nobody can read this slop. Nobody." He pulled a pen out of his pocket. "You go in my office and write this over again so that I can read it, and when you've done that, you come back out and I'll take another look."

Trent stood stock-still for a moment. I thought it might be over right then and there, but he took O'Leary's pen, and while we shot lay-ins, I could see him at O'Leary's desk, head down, rewriting his letter of apology. Finally he came out, handed the apology to O'Leary again.

"That's something like it," O'Leary grumbled, after he'd read the letter slowly and carefully. "Although whoever taught you handwriting should return his paycheck to the state." He looked up. "All right then, that's over with. Get out there and play." As Trent hustled onto the court, O'Leary shouted after him. "And keep that mouth of yours shut!"

You look back at little things and wonder if maybe they aren't so little. I was absolutely certain that was the first time Trent had ever apologized to anyone in his life, and O'Leary had made him do it twice. Looking at Trent, you could see that inside he was all torn up, afraid he'd lost face. It wouldn't have taken much to set him off, and if there'd been a second blowout, it would have been the last one.

It was an important day of tryouts. O'Leary had put my team up against a team that had Carver, Fabroa, and McShane. No more than a minute into the game Trent ripped down a defensive rebound. He fed me with a quick outlet, exactly the way Coach O'Leary wanted. I raced the ball right up the center of the court. Luke filled the lane on my left and Trent was on my right.

I could have fed Luke. He was open, and he'd had a big game the day before. But Trent was open too, and he deserved the ball. Or maybe I should say he needed the ball. I feathered a soft pass to him.

He soared for the lay-in. The ball hung on the lip of the rim, and for a second I wasn't sure it was going to drop. But then it did, and once that ball went through the hoop, it was as if the knots that had been tying him up were suddenly cut. He gave me his crooked smile—something I never thought would come my way.

After that Trent ran the court like a demon, crashed the boards harder than ever, and swished the jump shot I'd seen him practicing in the moonlight. With Luke hot from behind the three-point stripe, and with me dishing out assists to both of them, we steamrolled those varsity guys, controlling the court and everything that happened on it. Our dominance was so complete that Matt Markey actually went after Luke, fouling him hard on a breakaway and then standing over him, fists clenched, glowering. But Luke played it cool, simply standing up and walking away, making Markey looking so foolish that O'Leary laughed.

As we walked home on Friday, Luke turned to me. "What do you think, Nick? He can't cut us, can he?"

"No way," I said. "We're a lock."

He grinned. "I think so too. But I can hardly wait until Monday."

We talked about O'Leary for a while, and what it would be like to play for him. Then Luke brought up Trent. "I think he'll make the team, thanks to you. You made him look like a star, and O'Leary likes his aggressiveness."

"He's good enough, but he flunked a whole bunch of classes last year, and he's flunking a whole bunch this year. You can't play if you don't pass, can you?"

Luke shook his head. "Not where I came from."

Dad came by Sunday. He took me to the Kaddyshack Driving Range in Lynnwood. Neither of us is any good at golf, so we hacked away at the balls and talked. While we were hitting our second buckets, I told him I thought I'd made the team.

"What do you mean '*You think*'?"

"I won't know for sure until Monday. That's when they post the roster."

He tilted his head. "You know already, Nick. A player always knows. So did you make it, or didn't you?"

I swallowed. "I made it."

He reached over and rubbed the top of my head. "That's my boy!" Then, in a more serious tone, he continued: "You remember what I said about the final shot. If you get the chance, you step up and take it. Don't be thinking that just because you're a sophomore you've got to pass to some senior. You be the man."

After we finished hitting golf balls, we ate fish and chips at the Ivar's at Bothell Landing. I hoped we'd do something after lunch, maybe bike the trail again, but he drove me home. "I've got to talk to your mom," he said after we stepped inside the front door. "Business."

I climbed upstairs and turned on the Sonics-Kings game. But underneath the play-by-play I could hear the two of them arguing about support payments and lawyers. After about an hour, I heard the pick-up drive off. He hadn't even said goodbye.

Chapter 9 I made the team. When I saw my name

on the list, I felt exhilarated, but it wasn't like winning a million dollars. Dad had been right — a guy does know where he belongs. As Luke and I stared at the list, it was as if we were both checking on something that we knew had to be.

We'd stared at our names for a minute when I spotted

Trent's name at the bottom of the page with an asterisk after it. "What do you think that means?"

"Grades, I'll bet. Just like you thought."

"You think he'll hit the books now? Somehow I can't see Dawson studying."

Luke shrugged. "Give the guy some credit. You never thought he'd stick through tryouts, either."

Practice was different from tryouts, and it wasn't just that there were twelve guys where there had been thirty. During tryouts, O'Leary had stood back and watched us play. At practice he had every minute orchestrated. The run-and-gun showtime stuff was over. We stretched; we ran; we did passing and fast-break drills. Then came a chalk talk.

O'Leary knew the game in a way that no other coach I'd ever had knew it. *Double-downs, rotation to the ball, weakside help*—he explained all those things you hear about on television but don't really understand. And he explained not only what they were, but also how to do them.

When the chalk talk ended, we walked through the plays we'd learned. Then we had a controlled scrimmage—which means he blew the whistle every time somebody made a mistake, which was about every ten seconds. After that we ran more fast-break drills, had another chalk talk, and ran some more. We hardly had time to breathe, let alone think, before O'Leary was saying: "All right, gentlemen, that's it for today. Remember, on time tomorrow and every day. No excuses."

During practice Trent had had to do all the grunt work— the stretching, the running, the fast-break drills. When it came to the fun part, the actual scrimmaging, he was off to the side, forgotten, used only when somebody needed a rest. It made sense. He wasn't eligible, so why waste precious practice time on him? Still, it had to be rough.

And what happened after practice had to be rough, too. As soon as O'Leary blew the whistle, he led Trent into his office and sat him down at the desk in there. While the rest of us showered and shot the breeze, Trent was in that little room — still wearing his gym clothes — doing his schoolwork. When Luke and I walked out of the locker room and across the gym to go home, he was still there, sitting in his sweats with his head over a book.

I went home, ate some dinner, did my homework. By nine-thirty I was beat, absolutely exhausted. I lay on my bed and turned on the radio, too tired to do anything else. And it was right about then that I heard a basketball being dribbled in the back yard, heard Steve Clay and Trent talking in their low voices.

I was amazed. Where did Trent find the energy? I don't know how long they stayed that night, or on the other nights either. Not even the constant *thump, thump, thump* of a basketball on concrete could keep me awake.

Chapter 10 Our opening game was on a Thursday in early December. By the end of practice on Tuesday my legs were totally dead. As we dressed in the locker room I moaned to Luke about all the running O'Leary was having us do. "You'd think we were on a track team."

"It's a good sign for us," Luke said softly.

"What do you mean?" I asked, my voice dropping to a whisper.

"Simple. Last year's team always walked the ball up the court and ran a set offense. They weren't a running team. Right?"

"Yeah. That's true. But so what?"

"Don't you get it? O'Leary's changing his style. Fabroa can't run like you can; Matt Markey can't keep up with me. If we play up-tempo ball, those guys are on the bench and we're on the court."

My pulse quickened. "You really think so?"

"I know so. If we show O'Leary we can handle the pressure, we'll be first string by the end of the week."

I'd been figuring to play six or eight minutes a game. But Luke was talking about more. And why not? In my heart I knew I was better than Fabroa, that Luke was better than Markey. So what if they were seniors? Those guys had had their chance last year, and they'd done nothing with it. Ten wins, twelve losses. It was our turn.

"You ready?" Luke said.

I laced up my second shoe. "Yeah. Let's go."

As we left the locker room, I looked over to the coaches' office. But instead of seeing Trent with his head over some book, I saw a policeman sitting at O'Leary's desk, his nightstick jutting out from his hip. Trent was talking, and as he talked he was shaking his head back and forth vigorously. Both Luke and I stopped and stared. Coach O'Leary caught us staring, which immediately made us hustle out the door.

"I wonder what that was all about?" Luke murmured once we were outside.

When I reached home, there was more. "You missed all the excitement," Scott said as soon as I stepped inside.

"What are you talking about?"

"Zack Dawson. Two police cars came roaring up our block about an hour ago. It was quite a scene. One cop went around the back. The other knocked on the front door. They were inside for about ten minutes, then they led Zack away—in handcuffs. Mrs. Dawson was screaming at them from the front porch, calling them every name in the book. I'm telling you, it was something."

As he spoke I felt myself going pale. "What did he do?"

Scott shrugged. "How should I know? Stole something, probably. Or drugs. There are about a million things he could have done." He stopped, then looked at me. "What's wrong with you?"

"Nothing's wrong with me," I snapped, suddenly angry. "But there's something wrong with you. You act happy to see Zack get arrested."

His back stiffened. "Since when have you been big buddies with Zack Dawson? It seems to me a couple months ago he almost killed you."

"I'm not big buddies with Zack Dawson, or with Trent. But it doesn't make me happy to see them get in trouble. And I don't see why it should make you happy either."

I pushed past him and went to the kitchen, pulling the door closed behind me. I grabbed some Oreos and milk from the refrigerator, and then sat down and ate.

In eighth grade our class had gone on a field trip to the juvenile detention center. Before we'd gone, I'd figured the place would be a dump, with busted toilets and graffiti on the walls, like something from an old movie. But it was the opposite — spotlessly clean and modern, with a nice basketball court, a computer lab, a big library.

That was the first shock. The second was that the kids locked up in there didn't look that different from me. They were a little older, but not much. They wore orange jumpsuits and laughed loudly with one another as they moved from one room to the next. You could have told yourself they were having fun if it weren't for the double set of doors that locked them in and the guards that stood at those doors. Before we left the guides showed us the rooms the kids slept in. They were tiny little rooms, bare and cold. It spooked me to think that Zack was in one of those rooms.

I had to do something, so I went out to the basketball court. It felt good to pick up the basketball, to eye the hoop. I knocked down a three-pointer, retrieved the ball, and knocked down another one. That was more like it. I worked the ball between my legs, behind my back, controlling it as though it were a yo-yo on a string. I blocked out everything except the season coming up, the game on Thursday, and the minutes I was going to play.

After dinner I sat at my desk. Instead of doing my homework, I put my pencil down and listened to the sounds of the night. A car on 104th. A fire truck somewhere far off. Another car. Some dog, barking his fool head off. Something felt wrong.

Then it hit me. It wasn't any new sound that had thrown me off; it was a missing sound. Trent wasn't practicing with Steve Clay.

The Dawson house was shut up tight the next morning, and Trent wasn't at school either. Rumors floated around. Someone said Zack and Trent had been shooting a gun down by the trail. Somebody else said that they'd stolen a bunch of guitars from Mills Music. There was talk of broken windows at the school district offices, and swastikas painted on the outside of a synagogue in Redmond.

At practice Coach O'Leary stayed in his office while we ran through warm-ups. We could see him in there talking on the phone. When he finally came out, he called us together. "What do you bet Trent Dawson's no longer on this team?" Carver whispered as we shuffled over to O'Leary.

"You got that right," McShane agreed softly.

O'Leary's normally cheerful face seemed topsy-turvy. The corners of his mouth were down and his eyes drooped. He waited for absolute silence before he began.

"I won't beat around the bush. You know the police were here talking to Trent after practice yesterday. The long and the short of it is that they took him into custody. I spoke with Trent last night and again today, and he has given me his word that he has done nothing wrong. I accept his word, and I fully expect that when the investigation is over he will be cleared and that he will return to this team." He paused. "Any questions?"

Every one of us wanted to know *what* was being investigated, but nobody had the courage to ask.

"All right then," O'Leary said. "Let's get to work."

It was our last practice before the season started, and it was our worst. Guys were chirping at each other, acting more like opponents than teammates. Every time the gym door opened O'Leary stared toward it. When the two hours ended, it was like being released from the dentist's chair. Not exactly the way to start a season.

Part Three

Chapter 1 The next night, we opened the season against the Juanita Rebels at their gym. They had decent players at every position, and they had an all-star at guard, a six-four guy named Matthew Jefferson. When I played, I'd be guarding him.

There was no practice on game days, so as soon as school ended I walked straight home. Once I reached my block, I sneaked a peek over at the Dawson house. The shades were down; the curtains drawn. It looked like a house with a sick person in it.

When I opened the front door, Scott was sprawled out on the sofa, blowing into the mouthpiece of his trumpet. "Are they back?" he asked in a monotone.

"What?"

"Zack and Trent. I saw you staring at their house. Are they back?"

"Are you spying on me now?"

He gave me a pained look. "I'm sitting here on the sofa

looking out the window and I see you staring at the Dawson house for about five minutes. I wouldn't call that spying, would you? Now, are they back?"

"No, they're not."

I started toward the kitchen. "I heard what happened," he said, still using that irritating monotone. "I got it all from Katya. You interested?"

I turned back. "You know I am."

He stretched his arms above his head, yawned. "A couple of mornings ago a cyclist found some dead chickens and roosters down on the Burke-Gilman trail. They'd been clubbed with a baseball bat or something. It happened right where Zack and Trent hang out. The police asked around, and it turns out Michael Ushakov saw them do it."

"Michael did? Are you sure?"

Scott lowered his voice, as if someone might overhear. "Don't say anything to Katya, but this is where it gets tricky. You know Michael. Sometimes he says it was Zack. Sometimes he says it was Trent. Sometimes he says it was both of them."

I bit my lower lip. "What do you think will happen?"

"Who knows? Nothing, probably, unless they admit it. I can't see Michael testifying in court, can you?"

I shook my head. "No, I can't." Then, for the second time, I headed toward the kitchen.

"Dad called," Scott said.

Again I turned back. "What did he say?"

Scott shrugged. "Just that he'll be at the game."

"Nothing else?"

"I didn't pick up. The message is on the machine if you want to listen to it."

"What do you mean you didn't pick up?"

His face went red. "It's you he wanted to talk to, Nick, not me. I don't think it's even occurred to him that the band will be playing tonight."

We looked at each other for a long moment. Then he stuck the mouthpiece back into his trumpet and started flipping through his music book. A second later he was blowing on the horn, loud and clear.

Chapter 2 Mom came home early and stuck some
sort of pizza into the microwave for dinner. It wasn't a lot, which was perfect, because I was so nervous I couldn't have eaten much without puking.

Getting out to the car was a major production. First I forgot my basketball shoes. Then Scott had to go back inside for some sheet music. When Mom finally backed the car into the driveway, she realized she'd left her purse on the kitchen table. So it was back into the house one more time.

When I reached the locker room, my body felt incredibly cold. It was a raw December day, maybe forty degrees outside, with rain and wind, but the cold was from inside me. I wasn't alone. Nobody looked good. Not Luke, not Fabroa or Chang or Markey or McShane. Not even Carver.

Ten minutes before we were to take the court, Coach

O'Leary called us together. He was all business. "The Jefferson kid is the guy we have to contain. Notice I didn't say 'stop.' I said 'contain.' He's too good to be stopped. I'm not worried about his points, so long as he has to work for them. It's his defense that scares me. He's got long arms and good court sense. If they press us, don't loop passes over him. He'll pick them off and be dunking in your face. Guards, come back for the ball, dribble up the center of the court, and don't stop dribbling unless you've got someone to pass to. Forwards, stay out of the corners. Either drive straight to the basket or give up the ball to a guard so we can run a set play. Got it?"

The senior starters all said "Yeah!" real loud, while the rest of us croaked out a weaker version of the same word. "All right, let's go get 'em," O'Leary cried, clapping his hands.

During our lay-in and passing drills, I sneaked a peak into the stands. Right away I caught Dad's eye. He was beaming ear-to-ear and gave me two thumbs up. I looked for Mom then, but she wasn't there. For an instant I figured she must be buying food or drink or something, and then I remembered. They wouldn't be sitting together, not at this game, not at any game. She'd be on the other side of the gym, near the band and Scott. I wanted to wheel around and look for her, but I couldn't, not with O'Leary barking out last-minute instructions.

The horn sounded. The starters shuffled onto the court, acting as if they were in no hurry at all. I took a seat on the bench next to Luke, about halfway down.

You're not supposed to root against a guy on your own team, but it's hard to be riding the pines and not have some negative thoughts creep in. Carlos Fabroa had the job I wanted. If he did well, I was going to sit. But if he struggled, I just might get a chance.

Fabroa did okay for the first few minutes, keeping his dribble alive until he could make the smart pass. But breaking a press a couple of times isn't the same as breaking it over and over.

Jaunita led by two near the end of the first quarter, when he made his first terrible pass, a rainbow lob that their center picked off. Immediately they were off to the races, with Jefferson taking a pass in stride and throwing down a thunderous one-handed jam that electrified the crowd and totally rattled Fabroa.

Fabroa took the in-bounds pass; the double-team came at him. He tried to split the defenders, but dribbled the ball off his knee. Two seconds later Jefferson nailed a three-point shot from the corner. In less than five seconds Juanita's two-point lead had grown to seven.

"Nick! Luke!" Coach O'Leary yelled down the bench. We both popped up. "Get in there for Fabroa and Markey. And make something happen."

My skin went completely dry as I knelt at the scorer's table waiting for the next dead ball. When I actually took the court, my knees felt like metal hinges holding together two rigid boards. The ref handed the ball to Luke, he in-bounded to me, and I was playing in my first varsity game.

There was no chance to ease into the game, not with Jefferson guarding me. I drove hard to my right, lost him a little when I went behind my back with my dribble, and then cut straight toward the hoop. Carver's man rotated to me, and I made a bounce pass to Darren for the lay-in. Then I was back-pedaling, looking to pick up Jefferson, totally in the flow.

The rest of that half was like a track meet. Up and down the court we went, Juanita trying to disrupt our rhythm with their press, while we tried to make them pay for it with aggressive drives to the hoop. When the halftime buzzer sounded, we were up 36–32, and I still hadn't come out.

O'Leary kept both Luke and me out there to start the second half. I wanted to show him he was right to do it, but Jefferson was bigger than I was, and stronger. Toward the middle of the third quarter Juanita started posting me up. Jefferson would take the entry pass, everybody would clear out, and then he'd methodically back me down toward the hoop. When he had me where he wanted me, he'd give me a little pump fake or two, and then either spin by me or shoot over me. They scored on three out of four possessions using that same play, and twice I fouled him.

It was the fouls that stuck me on the bench at the start of the fourth quarter. That and the fact that I was so tired I was late getting back on defense. Luke came out with me, and we sat side-by-side, sweat dripping off us, watching.

The score was knotted at 57 when we left the floor. Nothing terrible happened, no 10–0 run or anything, but little by little Juanita pulled away. A three-point lead became five, then seven. With four minutes left their coach took Jefferson out, figuring the game was wrapped up.

Still Luke and I sat.

They led 68–58 with under three minutes left when Luke

and I finally returned. Two things made me think we still could win. I felt fresh, and Luke had that look in his eyes. Besides, the Juanita guys thought they had the game. They'd stopped pressing, and they weren't being careful with the ball. Jefferson was leaning back on the bench smiling, taking congratulations from fans in the first row, waiting for the clock to run out.

They didn't know about Luke's hot streaks. He caught fire right when we needed it, and I fed him the ball just the way you'd feed a campfire. He filled the basket. A three-pointer from the corner. A driving, spinning lay-in. A miss from the top of the key. But then two more three-pointers, both from well outside the arc. By the time the Juanita coach finally got a time out, we were up 75–74 and it was our fans, and our band, that was raising the roof.

Jefferson came back in, along with the other first-stringers, rested, but also out of sync. They hadn't expected to return; in their minds they were at the pizza parlor telling their girl-friends about all the shots they'd made.

The momentum was ours, but we just couldn't put them away. Our lead was three, then five, then three, then one: 83–82. That was the score when, with less than a minute left, Chang was open for a three-pointer from the corner. I hit him with a perfect pass and he went up in rhythm. In the air the shot looked good. I was certain it was going to be the dagger to the heart, but the ball hit the back rim and bounded high into the air. Juanita's center snatched the rebound, called time out, and it was anybody's game.

We huddled around O'Leary. I could see him eyeing me,

see the worry in his eyes. He looked toward Fabroa. Was he going to take me out? He couldn't. I had to finish the game. I had to! He coughed, then motioned for me to come closer. I was staying in.

"Listen up," O'Leary said. "Somehow or other, they'll get the ball to Jefferson. Nick, you get out on him, you hear me? Make sure he puts the ball on the floor and drives to the hoop. No open jumpers. Understand?

"Now for the rest of you. As soon as Jefferson puts the ball on the floor, I want whoever is closest to rotate off his man and double-team. If you're not sure it's you, go after him. Even a triple-team is okay by me. If Jefferson makes the good pass, and some other guy makes the shot, then I'll tip my cap to them and say good game. But I don't want Jefferson beating us. Make him pass the ball." The horn sounded. We headed back to the court. "And box out!" O'Leary yelled after us. "No second chances."

Just as O'Leary had predicted, Juanita worked a screen to get the ball to Jefferson on the right side, about eighteen feet from the hoop. Once Jefferson had the ball, they cleared out the side, setting it up for him to work me one-on-one.

Jefferson dropped both shoulders low and swung the ball in front of me. My eyes were locked on the ball as he moved it side to side. But my mind was going, too. He was good, but not so good that he'd try to make a long jumper at that moment. I backed off a little, just six inches, to give myself an edge when he did finally put the ball on the floor, in case I didn't get the double-team help. I didn't want him dunking in my face.

Then it happened, quicker than quick. The instant Jefferson saw me back off, he rose for his jumper. Awkwardly I lunged toward him, but I was too late to get a hand in his face; too late to bother his shot at all.

I'll never forget his eyes. They were incredibly intense, totally focused on the hoop. His release was perfect, the spin on the ball was perfect, the arc was perfect. Swish! Nothing but net. He drained that shot as though he was playing horse with his buddies in mid-July.

I looked to our bench. O'Leary had his hands in the air, his eyes were closed, and his face was contorted with pain. "No! No! No!" he was shouting. Juanita had the lead back with seventeen seconds left.

We had no time-outs. Luke in-bounded to me. A feeling of panic, of desperation, overcame over me. I'd blown it!

I brought the ball across the center line, my heart racing. Jefferson came out on me, picked me up. Carver clapped his hands, calling for the ball, but I wasn't giving it up. *"Be the man."* That's what my dad had said. Jefferson had burned me; now I was going to scorch him.

I turned my back to the basket and started backing Jefferson down, bumping against him, working closer and closer to the hoop. Luke flashed into the key, looking for a pass, but I let him go. This was me against Jefferson.

I could hear the crowd counting down the seconds. *Eight ... seven ... six ... five ...* I gave Jefferson my best head fake. He didn't bite. I gave him another one, and another. Still, he held his ground. *Three ... two. ...* In desperation I turned baseline, hoping to get off a fade-away jumper. But he was all over me. I couldn't jump, couldn't even see the basket. All I saw was his hand. Still I released the ball.

It went about an inch. Then Jefferson stuffed the ball right back in my face, stuffed me so hard I fell flat on my back, the ball landing on my belly as I fell.

The horn sounded. Juanita fans rose in a great roar of happiness. The Juanita players hugged Jefferson and then high-fived each other. I closed my eyes and lay there, hoping that when I opened them it would turn out to have been a bad dream.

In the locker room after the game none of the other guys said a word, but I knew what they were thinking. That I'd blown it, that I'd made a sophomore's play, an idiot's play, and had cost us the game, the league opener. I relived that last minute over and over. All the mistakes! Backing off Jefferson. Not passing to Carver. Not passing to Luke. Trying to do it all myself! Who did I think I was?

The locker room emptied. Still I sat, unable to rouse myself. O'Leary left, not even saying goodbye. I remembered the final huddle, the way he'd looked at me and then looked at Fabroa. He'd given me my chance. Right away, in the opening game, he'd put the team in my hands. And I'd choked. I'd choked big time.

Dad drove me home. "What were you thinking?" he said, slapping the steering wheel as he spoke. "Trying to back a guy like that down and shoot over him? No way, Nick. You've got to drive on someone like that, use your quickness against him. Drive to the hoop or stop and take the pull-up jumper, but not back him down. Use your head, or the coach is going to sit your butt down." He pulled up in front of the house. I got out, and he leaned across and rolled down the window. "You get only so many chances, Nick. You've got to play smart."

Chapter 3 At lunch on Friday Luke and I sat off by ourselves. "You made a couple of bad plays," he said. "It happens. You'll get another chance."

"Yeah," I mumbled. "Next year."

He laughed. "Come on. Fabroa can't play the whole game. You've got to get some minutes. Play your game tomorrow night against Eastlake and you'll be okay."

In the locker room before practice it was as if I had some contagious disease. Even Luke left me alone. I dressed in the corner, then headed out, head down.

But the court worked its magic. I stepped on the hardwood and it was like coming home. All the drills — passing, shooting, rebounding — were like old friends. Luke was right: there'd be another game, another chance.

With an hour left in practice, O'Leary blew his whistle. My throat tightened. Scrimmage. Would he say something to me? Point out my mistakes to everybody? Or would he let it go?

We gathered around him. He took out a red handkerchief and wiped the sweat from his forehead. "All right, listen up. I want to go over some changes for tomorrow's game." He looked at Brian Chang. "Brian, Luke Jackson is going to take your spot on the starting unit. But don't worry, you'll be the first guy off the bench."

Chang flushed. "Sure, Coach. Whatever you say."

"Good. Good attitude. The kind of attitude I like to see. The kind that wins games. Which brings me to my next point." O'Leary paused, and when he spoke there was anger in his voice. "We were too wild against Juanita, too helter-skelter. From now on, if the lay-in isn't there on the fast break, pull the ball out and run a play. No more playground stuff. Everybody got it?"

I got it all right. He might as well have pointed right at me. I was the playground guy, the point guard who didn't run set plays.

"All right, then, let's walk through our plays. I want the first team on the court, and I want the rest of you along the wall watching. We're going to do it until we get it right."

I found a spot by the drinking fountain and watched. Or pretended to watch. When it was the second team's turn to be on the court, I did everything O'Leary asked, but I did it the way a zombie might. "Get with it, Abbott!" O'Leary bellowed more than once. I couldn't free my mind from Juanita's gym; I kept reliving that final minute. If I'd stayed tight on Jefferson. If I'd passed the ball to Carver or Luke.

The whistle finally blew. "All right, that's it for today," O'Leary shouted. "Shower up."

I headed for the locker room.

"Abbott," O'Leary called, "could I see you for a minute?"

As I followed him into his office, my heart pounded. What now? A one-on-one chewing out?

O'Leary closed the door behind us, then rubbed his freckled

hands together. "I know this was a tough day for you, Nick."

My throat was so tight I wasn't sure I could breathe.

He waited, but when he saw I wasn't going to answer, he went on. "I won't pretend I liked the way you played last night. You forgot about your teammates, forgot about your coach, tried to do it all yourself. But I take the blame for putting you in that position. Point guard is the toughest job on the court. You weren't ready for it, not after a couple of weeks of practice, and I should have known that."

"I'll do better next time," I managed to say. "I've thought about what I did, and I know I'll do better."

"Good. That's what I wanted to hear. Be patient. Don't force things. Let the game come to you."

A little flame of hope came to life inside me. "Coach, if you give me another chance, I won't screw up again. I promise."

He smiled. "That's the spirit. It's a long season. You'll get your chance."

I thought he was done. I started for the door, but before I could leave he called me back. "There's something else I want to talk to you about, Nick." The tone of his voice was strange, and so was the expression on his face. He cleared his throat. I waited. "Teammates help each other out, both on and off the court. That's true, don't you think?"

"Sure, Coach," I answered.

He drummed his fingertips on his desk. "So, that brings us to Trent Dawson."

"Trent Dawson?" I stammered.

"You live across the street from him, don't you?"

"Yeah, but I don't see him much. He keeps to himself."

O'Leary nodded. "What I'm going to tell you now is confidential. I can trust you, can't I?"

"Sure, Coach. You don't have to worry about me."

"Okay, then. I talked with the cop handling Trent's case. They've charged that brother of his with eight counts of animal cruelty." O'Leary scowled. "Killing little baby ducks and geese, for God's sake. They should lock the S.O.B. up and throw away the key, but they won't, of course. I had him in gym class two years ago and . . ." He stopped midsentence, waving his hand above his head. "Listen to me, I'm rambling on like a crazy man. The important thing is that Trent had nothing to do with it. He's been released from the juvenile detention center. He's home now, or at least he should be. That's where you come in. I want you to check on him."

I flushed. "I'm glad he's not in any trouble, but Trent and I aren't exactly friends. In fact, I think he half-hates me."

O'Leary smiled. "I've looked through Trent's school records. If he only half-hates you, you're not doing bad. It looks to me as if he completely hates just about everybody else." He stared at me. When I didn't speak, he went on. "I'm not asking you to marry him, Nick. All I want you to do is knock on the door and see if he's there."

I swallowed. "I'll check on him, Coach. But what do I say if he is home?"

"Tell him to be at our game tomorrow, and at practices next week. Tell him the team is counting on him for the second half of the season. Tell him we need him."

"You want me to tell him that?"

O'Leary caught the disbelief in my question. His eyes honed in on me. "I certainly do. Because we do need him. We need his toughness, his aggressiveness. I've been coaching a long time, Nick, a long time. A team is like a jigsaw puzzle. Trent is one of the pieces. Just as you are. We need all the pieces."

I nodded. "I'll tell him."

O'Leary stood. "All right. That's it, then."

It was a simple request. All I had to do was walk across the street and give Trent's front door two raps. If Trent wasn't there or didn't answer, then I'd just walk back to my house. If he did answer, then I'd tell him what Coach had said. Either way the whole thing wouldn't take more than two minutes.

Still I put it off and put it off. I ate dinner and afterwards returned to my room to listen to the Sonics game. But I couldn't concentrate. I flicked off the radio and went downstairs. "Where are you going?" Mom asked when she saw I was heading outside.

I explained.

"Well, you deliver the message and then you come right back. I don't want you spending any more time with him than you have to."

"Don't worry about that," I said, lacing up my shoes. "This isn't my idea."

Rain had started to fall. I crossed the street quickly, climbed his porch steps, took a deep breath, and knocked. I could hear voices inside, Ericka Dawson's and Steve Clay's. They sounded hateful, the way Mom's and Dad's voices had sounded just before Dad moved out. I thought about knocking again, but decided against it. I'd turned and was heading down the stairs when Trent opened the door.

He looked terrible. He had on a ripped T-shirt, dirty sweats, and no shoes. His hair was sticking up as if it hadn't been combed in a week. "What do you want?" he muttered.

"I don't want anything. I'm just here to deliver a message."

"What message?"

"Coach O'Leary sent me. He wants you to know that you're still on the team, that he's counting on you for the second half of the season. He wants you at the game tomorrow and at school and practice next week."

From inside the house I heard his mother's voice. Her words were slurred, as if she'd been drinking. "Trent. Who is it? Is that the police?"

"It's nobody," he called back to her.

"Then close the door. You're letting the heat out."

"Yeah, yeah," he answered. He looked back to me. For a moment I thought he might say something.

"Trent, close the damn door!" his mother shrieked.

"All right!" he shouted back, and then he did close it, right in my face.

When I returned, Mom wanted to hear what had happened. "What do you think he's going to do?" she asked when I'd finished.

"I don't know."

"Steve Clay? Was he there?"

I almost told her about the shouting in the background,

but decided to let it drop. "I didn't see him, but I heard his voice."

She pursed her lips. "At least he's still living there. He's the only stable influence in that house." I headed toward the stairs and my room. "Nick," she called after me, "I forgot to ask how practice went."

"It was fine," I said. "No problems."

Around ten o'clock I heard it, the sound of a basketball on concrete. When I looked out the window, there was Trent, in the night rain, playing basketball. He was alone, but he played with the fire you bring to a championship game: driving the lane, pump faking invisible defenders, snatching rebounds, whirling this way and that.

Most people would have thought he looked ridiculous, and I guess he did. But I knew what he was doing. He was playing imaginary games in his mind, the same way I had on many a summer afternoon at Canyon Park. Only for him it was different, because when I'd played my imaginary games, it was only Scott I destroyed. Trent was taking on the world.

Chapter 4 When Trent, neatly dressed in jeans and a T-shirt, entered the locker room before the Eastlake game on Saturday, I was the only one who wasn't stunned. Even O'Leary looked as if he'd seen a ghost, though he recovered fast. He went over to Trent and shook his hand. "Good to have you back, Son."

After that, the normal locker-room noise slowly returned.

Or almost returned. Guys would talk about the game coming up, but out of the corners of their eyes they'd glance at Trent, wondering if he'd really killed those birds, and what it was like to spend time in jail.

Then there was no time to worry about Trent. O'Leary called us together for the final chalk talk. He repeated everything he'd said at practice. We were going to the set offense. No fast breaks unless we had clear numbers. A game plan perfect for Fabroa.

As we went through the warm-up drills, I looked up into the stands. I spotted my father right away. When our eyes met, he made a fist to encourage me. My stomach turned over. What was I going to say to him if I ended up riding the bench for the whole game?

I moved to the front of the lay-up line. The ball came to me, and I took a couple of hard dribbles, rose, banked in a lay-in, then jogged to the end of the line. That's when I saw the band.

Scott was in the center; Katya right next to him. My mother was sitting a few rows above them, swaying back and forth, clapping her hands, totally caught up in the music as Scott pointed his trumpet right, left, up, down, playing "YMCA" better than I've ever heard it played, making the whole gym rock. The horn sounded. Game time.

In the opener I'd had Luke next to me, but now I was alone. While I sat on the bench, he was out on the court, running the lanes and hitting the pull-up jump shots. After a hoop he'd smile at Fabroa, and Fabroa would give him a little nod, and it was as if I didn't exist. Carver was hitting his shots, too; in fact the whole team was clicking. We jumped off to a 6–0 lead, then 12–5. We were up 16–11 with a minute left in the quarter before Fabroa finally came out and I stepped onto the court.

"Be patient," I whispered to myself as I took the court, and I was. We had two possessions in that minute. On one we scored, on the other McShane turned the ball over. I was back on the bench when the second quarter started, not a drop of sweat on me. Killing time, not making mistakes, filling in so Fabroa could rest — was that going to be my season?

Eastlake pulled even as Fabroa struggled through the second quarter. He threw the ball away twice and missed all three shots he took. I could do better. I knew it, and I wanted to show it. Still I heard O'Leary's voice. *Don't force things. Let the game come to you.*

Right before halftime I got the call again. And again I played it safe. I passed up a jumper on the fast break only to see Markey miss a sweeping hook in the key. I had a chance for a steal, but held back, and Eastlake eventually scored on a drive to the hoop by their shooting guard. When the horn sounded I had no turnovers, no assists, and no points.

When the third quarter started, I was riding the pines again. The lead seesawed back and forth. Time after time I saw fast break opportunities, opportunities that Fabroa passed up. I wanted to burst. If I'd been on the court playing my game, we'd have pulled away from them.

I got my minute at the end of the quarter. One lousy, useless minute. Eastlake had the ball when I came on, and they held it for about thirty seconds before they scored on a bank shot by their center. I brought the ball down, passed to Markey, who backed the ball in before missing a turnaround jumper. The Wolves came back, ran more clock, and scored with three seconds left. As the horn sounded ending the quarter, I was throwing up a wild air ball from half court. It was my first shot of the game.

For a while I didn't think I would play again. Luke caught fire and drained back-to-back three-pointers, giving us a four-point lead. But with about four minutes left, Fabroa stopped looking for Luke or McShane, and instead dumped the ball into Carver time and again. Eastlake's defense double-teamed, then covered his passing lanes, shutting us down completely. Just like that, the Wolves went on an 8–0 run to take back the lead.

O'Leary called time out. His eyes were like lasers. "Don't force it!" he shouted at Fabroa. "If Darren is covered swing it to somebody else." But the next time down Fabroa tried to dump it into Carver again. Eastlake tipped the ball free, and they were off to the races for another easy bucket. Worse, Fabroa fouled after the shot.

O'Leary grabbed the top of his head with both hands. I thought he was going to pull out the little hair he had left. "Abbott! Get in there!"

As I stepped onto the court, my heart was pumping blood by the gallon. It was the home opener, the league opener. The gym was rocking. My mom, dad, and brother were watching.

The Eastlake player swished the free throw. I took the in-bound pass and raced the ball up the court. The guy guarding me backed off, looking to clog the passing lanes. I rose for the three-pointer. It felt good when I released it, but I must have been too pumped, because it clanged long. *That's all right,* I thought to myself as I back-pedaled. *You'll make the next one.*

But that miss took away my confidence. My man gave a simple head fake. I bit, and he blew by me for a lay-in. As I brought the ball upcourt, I saw O'Leary pacing in front of the bench, his hands behind his neck, dark half-moons of sweat showing on his light blue shirt. He had the same look on his face that he'd had just before he yanked Fabroa.

I picked up my dribble at the top of the key. I faked a pass to Carver; Luke flashed into the key. I fed him a lob pass that he took at the free-throw line. My guy dropped into a double-team, so Luke whipped the ball right back. I was open for the three-pointer, but my hands were so sweaty the ball slipped, and my shot was ugly—a low-liner that sailed under the backboard and out of bounds.

"Air ball! Air ball! Air ball!" The mocking chant rose from the Eastlake fans. I felt my face go red as Eastlake quickly inbounded the ball. As my man raced up the right side of the court, I reached in, tipping the ball free. I barely nicked his arm, but the whistle blew and the ref's finger was pointing at me. A second later the horn sounded. Fabroa raced onto the court, and he was pointing at me, too.

O'Leary didn't even look at me as I came off the court. I grabbed a towel and, totally dejected, walked all the way down to the end of the bench. I dropped my head and covered it with a towel. That's when I felt the pat on the back, and the low, whispered words: "You'll get 'em next time."

We lost by ten. After the game my father took me home. I didn't want to eat anything, but he insisted we stop for pizza. While we sat waiting for our food, he let me have it, telling me everything I already knew: that I'd played like an idiot, that I was too tentative in the first half and too wild in the fourth quarter. "You've got to think when you're out there. You understand? You've got to think."

He reached over and rubbed the top of my head. He did that all the time when I was little, and I'd always liked it. But now he rubbed too hard, so that it hurt. Besides, I wasn't little anymore. I pulled away.

My mother had waited up. "You did your best, Nick. That's all you can do. No one can be great every time, not even Michael Jordan." Scott had the sense not to say anything.

Upstairs, staring at the ceiling, I kept seeing my mistakes. It was as if I were locked in a movie theater and were being forced to watch a gruesome clip from a horror film over and over. Then, just before I fell asleep, I let the film run a few seconds longer in my mind. I saw myself after I'd been taken out of the game. I was at the end of the bench, a towel over my head. Then I felt the pat on the back, and the words of comfort. *You'll get 'em next time.*

Could that have been Trent?

Chapter 5 Monday morning Luke was at my door. We didn't usually walk to school together, so I knew he'd come by to try to lift my spirits. For a while we talked about school—midterms were that week—and how hard it was to find time to study. Then the conversation turned to basketball.

"You're going to be okay, Nick. You're going to be okay."

"When?" I scoffed. "My senior year?"

"No, no. You've just got to become more of a team player."

His words stung. "What's that supposed to mean?"

He caught my tone. "Nothing...just..."

"Go on. If you got something to say, say it."

He shrugged. "Well, it seems like you're trying to do everything yourself when you're out there. You've got to remember you've got teammates who can score too."

My whole body tensed, but I kept myself under control. "And I suppose you don't care about scoring."

"Come on. You know what I mean. Everybody likes to score. But if it doesn't come to me, I don't force things."

"And I do? Is that what you're saying?"

"A little, you have been."

I exploded. "You've got a lot of nerve, Luke. I'll tell you, a lot of nerve. Because you count your points more than anybody I've ever played with."

"Oh, is that right?"

"Yeah, that's right."

He glared at me. "Fine, Nick. Keep doing things the way

you have been. You can sit on the bench all year for all I care." With that he stormed off, leaving me to myself.

All morning I thought about how unfair he was. You miss the big shot and you're a glory hog. You make it and suddenly you're the guy with courage, the guy willing to step up with the game on the line.

I'd always eaten lunch with Luke, and out of habit I looked for him that day too. But when I spotted him, he was in thick with Carver and the other senior starters. *Fine,* I thought, my anger returning. *You eat with them. See if I care.*

I had my history midterm that afternoon. I wasn't exactly unprepared for it, but I could have studied harder. When I finished my essay I looked up and saw everyone else — including Trent — still working. What a joke it would be if he ended up eligible to play and I flunked myself right off the team. I put my head down and went over my essay, checking for misspellings and lousy sentences, improving it wherever I could.

The school day ended and I walked to the gym for practice. I was tired of being on the outs with Luke. I needed a friend. If he'd done anything at all, even looked at me, I'd have gone over and made it okay with him. But the instant he saw me he turned away. I found an empty corner and suited up without saying a word to anybody.

We'd gone through all our warm-up drills and were getting ready for scrimmage when Coach O'Leary called me aside. "Listen, Nick," he said, his voice soothing, so soothing that I knew bad news was coming. "You're a good player. I know it; all the guys know it. But you're pressing."

"I'll play better," I said anxiously.

"Sure you will, sure you will. But for right now, I've decided to move you to the third team and let Brian Chang take your minutes. During the scrimmage today, I want you to sit up in the stands and watch. You can learn a lot from watching. You understand what I'm saying?"

It was like taking a fist to the gut and then having to act as if it hadn't hurt. I nodded, and even managed a sort of smile.

O'Leary put his hand on my shoulder. "Good, good. That's the attitude."

He blew his whistle and called the whole team to him. I could tell from the grin on Brian Chang's face that he knew he'd get my playing time. A couple of guys sneaked looks over at me, and I met their gazes as if nothing was wrong.

When you're scrimmaging, time always goes by fast. But when you're stuck watching, it's a whole different story. There were two of us sitting up on those hard bleachers: me and Trent. We sat as far apart from one another as we could, and didn't say a word.

The hardest part was knowing that neither Fabroa nor Chang had my ability. That's not bragging; it's just true. They weren't as fast; they didn't dribble as well; they didn't have my touch, inside or out. But during that practice they moved the ball around, keeping everybody involved. "That's it!" O'Leary called out a couple of times. "That's it!"

By Wednesday afternoon I knew there was no way I was getting into Thursday's game against the Redmond Mustangs. Not even for a minute.

Wednesday night I sucked up my courage and called Dad.

He answered, not his girlfriend, and that was something. But he didn't take what I had to tell him very well. "What do you mean you're not playing?"

"I'm third string. Unless it's a blowout I won't get in."

"What's going on, Nick? You arguing with the coach?"

"No, no. Nothing like that." I paused. "Look, Dad, there are only three sophomores on the team and I'm one of them. So I don't play a whole bunch this year. So what? I've got time."

There was a long stretch of silence. At last he spoke. "Well, thanks for telling me. I have the opportunity to work some overtime, and I might just take it. You keep playing hard at practice, you hear? And if anything changes, call me."

Chapter 6 Bench warmer. That's what I was for games three and four. I couldn't even kid myself that the guys needed me, because we won both games, beating Redmond at home 64–50 and then going on the road to stop the Lake Washington Kangaroos 56–44. Not that the victories meant much. They were the weakest teams in our league. No height, no speed, new coaches every year.

Fabroa and Chang ran the plays just the way O'Leary wanted them run: nothing flashy, but nothing stupid. They didn't blow either team out of the gym; they methodically ground them up the way a butcher grinds up meat to make sausage.

If we'd opened against these two loser teams, everything

might have been different. With less pressure, my shots might have dropped, and I might have made the plays on defense. If I had, then . . .

During those two games O'Leary didn't call my number once. I could have ordered a pizza and eaten it on the bench and he wouldn't have noticed.

Zack was released from juvenile hall the day after we beat Lake Washington. December in the Northwest is cold, dark, and drizzly, but he made a point of sitting on his porch every afternoon and evening, stereo blasting, cigarette in hand. It was as if he were flipping off the whole world.

The music didn't get turned down until Steve Clay came home, and then only after loud arguments that usually ended with Zack climbing into his mother's old Corolla and somehow making it sound like a Ferrari as he raced off into the night.

Katya was around our house more than ever those days, supposedly because of the jazz band, but really because she and Scott were an established thing. Like the rest of us, she tried to ignore Zack, but one evening when she stayed for dinner we heard him screaming in the street, and her frustration boiled over. "I don't understand," she said. "Why did they let him out? Michael saw him. He told the police. And nothing happens?"

My mother's voice was calm. "We don't know that for sure. He might have to do community service, or maybe undergo counseling. We don't know what the court decided."

"But he's there," Katya cried, pointing toward the Dawson house. "He's right *there,* and he's no different, and all those poor birds are dead."

No one could say anything to that.

Then, the night before Christmas vacation began, Steve Clay was at our door again. His face looked grayish, and the creases running by the sides of his mouth seemed deeper.

I let him in, called Mom, and slipped into the kitchen to listen. "You must be sick of seeing my face," he said softly as he sat, his back hunched.

"No, not at all," my mother answered. "What can I do for you?"

"Actually, I came over to say goodbye."

"Goodbye?"

He took a deep breath, sighed. "It didn't work out with Ericka and me. It's not Ericka's fault. It's just..." his voice trailed off.

"I'm sorry for you and for Ericka, and for the boys, too," my mother said. "You were good for them."

"It's the boys I want to talk to you about." He stopped for a moment. "Listen, this is the last time we'll ever talk, so I'm going to lay it all out. I got nowhere with Zack. Nowhere at all. But Trent's different. There's a chance for him. I'd like to think he had some place to go at night other than out with Zack. So I was wondering—"

"That basketball court is his whenever he wants to play," my mother said, anticipating his request. "You tell him that. And we've got a sofa downstairs to sleep on if he ever needs it. You tell him that too."

110

Steve Clay's spine straightened. "Thank you. Thank you very much. You're a good woman." He pulled out his wallet, wrote down a phone number on a scrap of paper. "I'm moving in with my brother. I won't be there for long, but if you ever need to get in touch with me, he'll know where I am."

My mother took the little piece of paper.

Steve Clay left, and my mother stood in the front room looking at the door. Finally she turned to me. "You heard that, didn't you? Is that okay?"

I remembered how angry I'd felt when she first allowed Trent to use my basket, but now I couldn't remember exactly why. "Sure," I said. "It's okay by me."

Chapter 7 We were entered in a three-day Christmas tournament in Victoria, British Columbia, beginning December 28. The games had popped right out at me the first time I'd seen the schedule. Riding the Victoria Clipper with the guys, staying in a hotel, seeing R-rated movies at night—the whole thing seemed great, almost like being a college player.

From the start Mom hadn't been crazy about the trip. She'd considered coming along as a chaperone because she didn't trust O'Leary. "I heard he's a drinker," she said one night at dinner. But Scott's jazz band was headed to Monterey, California, over Christmas for the music festival, and she wanted to go with him.

For a long time she stewed about it, then over Thanksgiving Dad solved the problem. "I'll go up with Nick, keep an eye on him," he told her. To me he said: "Don't worry. I'll stay out of your hair. You hang out with your buddies, not your old man."

School was out for the holidays, and there were no games until after Christmas, but that didn't mean time off. It was practice, practice, practice—twice a day. O'Leary called it our "readjustment" time. "We can make a run at the league title," he said. "But these practices are crucial. This is not playtime."

I wanted to use those practices to push Chang from his spot on the second team, and maybe make Fabroa nervous about his spot on the first team. I was going to show O'Leary that what he'd seen was a slump, and that it was over. But it didn't work out that way. At every practice something went wrong right away. I'd miss my first shot, or double-dribble, or make a bad pass. The harder I tried, the worse I did. If guys were open, I'd double-clutch on my passes, and then either chuck them out-of-bounds or get them picked off. It was like a rock slide that I once saw up in the Cascade mountains. First one rock came tumbling down, and then another, and pretty soon it seemed as if the whole mountain was caving in.

I hit bottom at our last practice before the trip. On a three-on-three fast break, I made a spin move in the key, then tried to swoop in a running lay-in. The ball somehow slipped out of my hands and bounced off my forehead and out-of-bounds. I must have looked like a total fool. O'Leary's eyes went to the roof. He crossed himself. "Jesus, Mary, and Joseph," he bellowed, "help me in my time of need!" All the guys roared with laughter, and I managed a smile, but the lump in my throat was so big I could hardly speak.

That happened on December 24. O'Leary phoned that night. He started out by wishing me a merry Christmas and asking me about my family and all that, but something was up. Finally there was a long pause. "About the trip to Victoria."

"What about it?" I asked.

He coughed. "You know how tight things are with school budgets and all. Well, it turns out that they raised the prices on the Victoria Clipper. Instead of having money for fifteen, we've only got money for twelve. That means ten players and me and Mr. Fabroa, who's going to help chaperone. You see what I'm saying?"

"I understand," I mumbled.

There was a long pause. "Look, Nick, I know you're disappointed. But you're a sophomore. The team makes a trip every year over Christmas. You'll get your chance."

Once he hung up, Mom asked who I'd been talking to. I lied, telling her it was Luke. "I haven't seen much of him lately," she said. "Is he coming over?"

"No," I said. "He's got family things."

Christmas morning Scott and I opened our gifts early: clothes, CD's, the usual stuff. Without Dad there, it felt all wrong. Around noon he did stop by. Still, it wasn't like a real Christmas. He sat on the sofa in his normal spot, only he never kicked off his shoes, never even leaned back into the cushions. He didn't look any more comfortable than the insurance agent who'd come by to update my mother's policies.

After about an hour he stood to leave. I followed him outside. "I got some bad news yesterday," I said. Immediately his eyes registered worry. "It's about basketball."

"What happened?"

I blurted it out. "They just don't have enough money to bring everybody on the team to Victoria, so I'm not going."

His eyes flared in anger. "Tell O'Leary I'll pay the fare, if that's all it is."

I winced. "That's nice of you and everything, but I wouldn't want to go like that. You see what I mean?"

He thought for a minute. "Yeah, I see what you mean." He paused. "Are you telling me everything, Nick? You're not feuding with the coach or anything, because if—"

"No, Dad," I interrupted. "It's nothing like that. I'm just not playing well. I'm trying, but nothing is going right."

"Well, all you can do is try."

There was no anger in his voice, no disappointment even. It was as if he'd given up on me. He pulled his keys out of his pocket. "I should be going now. Merry Christmas, Nick."

Chapter 8 We had our own little Christmas dinner: Scott, Mom, and me. Ham, mashed potatoes, asparagus, and for dessert pumpkin pie with whipped cream. There was nothing wrong with it, but there was nothing right with it either. I kept thinking about when I was younger—five, six, seven. Then two of my grandparents were still alive. The table was so crowded with food and people that we had had to put the extra leaf in. And the house, too, was full of sounds. My grandfather's transistor radio always on to the news, the jangling bracelets on my grandmother's arm. Now they were both dead, and my father was gone. My whole world seemed to be shrinking.

After dinner I told Mom about Victoria. She was upset at the thought of my being alone. "You come with us to Monterey. I can get another ticket."

But I knew how worried she was about money. Besides, the idea of seeing Scott on stage was too much for me. The way things were coming together for him just reminded me how everything was falling apart for me. "I'll be sixteen this summer. I can spend a few days alone. And if I need anything, I can always call Dad."

She thought. "You could stay at your dad's place. If you want, I'll ask."

"I don't want to stay there," I said, wondering if she knew about his live-in girlfriend. "I'll be fine here."

We talked some more about it, until she finally came around. But she hugged me tight when the airport shuttle arrived at our door early the next morning. "I'll call every night," she said.

Scott grinned at me. "Hey, Nick, now you can have one of those wild parties that make the newspaper. You know: Bothell Police Arrest..."

"That will be enough of that," my mother said, and I could tell she didn't think Scott was being the least bit funny. Then they were down the walkway and into the van.

"Good luck!" I shouted to Scott as the door closed.

115

Once they were gone, the house seemed wrong, as if it were a stranger's. When I took a cup down from the cabinet, it clattered on the counter. When I closed a door, the sound echoed loudly, as if I were in a museum. The background sounds of the house, sounds like my mother typing on her computer or Scott practicing his trumpet, were all absent.

Outside a light rain was falling. I turned on the television and tried to watch a movie, but my mind kept wandering. I turned the movie off, stuck in a Sonics video, but even that didn't help. The announcer was screaming about some tremendous dunk, but there was nothing inside me to match his excitement.

Time crawled by. I had to force myself to eat lunch. The mail came. Three catalogs—two for clothes and one filled with Valentine stuff.

Around four my mother phoned. They were in the hotel in Monterey. It was windy, but the sun was shining, and the coast of California was incredibly beautiful. She put Scott on. The band was going to compete the next morning, go to the aquarium in the afternoon, then take a night cruise in the bay. "They say there might be whales."

I ate a TV dinner, or half of it, then went to my room and turned on the radio. The Washington Huskies were at Wisconsin, up by six at the start of the second half. I listened for a few minutes, then flicked the radio off. I thought about calling Dad, but I didn't have anything to say to him. Besides, his girlfriend might have answered, and I definitely didn't want to talk to her. I turned off the light and lay on my bed in the dark, listening to the silence. That's when I heard the gate creak open and the bouncing ball.

In the summer, I'd been the one playing ball all the time. Trent had been the loser, the quitter who walked off the court whenever his brother showed up. Now he was playing basketball every minute he wasn't studying, and I was spending my time turning the television off and on, flipping through catalogs, and generally doing nothing. When he became eligible—and he'd make it, with all the studying he'd done—he'd move ahead of me in O'Leary's rotation. I'd be the last guy at the end of the bench.

My body was settled into the soft bed. My stereo was right there. If I turned it on, I could block Trent out, block basketball out, block everything out.

There are moments in your life when you know you've got to go in one direction or another. I took a deep breath, exhaled. Then I pulled myself off the bed, changed into my sweats, and tramped downstairs and out the back door.

When Trent saw me he jumped back as if he'd seen a ghost. It took a second, but then I realized what had happened: I'd scared him. The lights were out in my house. He must have figured the place was empty, that I was in Victoria, and that my mom and Scott were gone, too.

"You mind if I shoot around with you?" I asked.

It was a crazy question. He was in my back yard shooting at my hoop. Then again, maybe it wasn't so crazy. Because once night fell the court became his, and I was the outsider.

"Sure," he said. "You can play."

In the pale moonlight the basket seemed only half real, half there. You'd think that the darkness would make it hard to shoot, but it actually helped me concentrate. There was nothing else to see, nothing else to hear. O'Leary wasn't shouting instructions at me; my dad wasn't scrutinizing my every move. There was just the basket in front of me, the ball in my hands, and Trent defending.

But in a way that's not even right. Because it wasn't Trent. Or at least not the Trent I knew, the tough-guy Trent, the Trent who'd knock you down as soon as look at you. There were none of the pointless shoves, none of the mean-spirited fouls, none of the trash-talk that marked his game.

Not that he didn't play tough. He guarded me tight on defense and he came at me hard on offense. I did the same to him. But everything was *fair.* It was the purest game of basketball I've ever played, so pure that neither of us ever thought of keeping score.

If we hadn't tired I think we would have played all night. But finally, on a stutter-step, he dribbled the ball off his foot. It rolled into the bushes, and neither of us made a move to go get it. "Enough," he said.

"Enough," I replied.

I went inside and got a liter of Pepsi and brought it out. I suppose I could have invited him in, but I didn't want to leave the darkness. We drank in silence for a few minutes.

"That was a good game," I said.

"Yeah," he answered. "It was."

He took another swig, then stood to leave. "How about tomorrow night?" I asked. "You want to play again?"

"Okay. Tomorrow night."

Chapter 9 The next morning I woke up filled with energy. I made myself breakfast, then went out to the shed and dug out the painting stuff. The paint in the downstairs bathroom was peeling. It was supposed to be a creamy white, but you could see the pink and yellow that had been underneath.

My father had always said he was going to repaint. He actually bought the paint, but he never got around to it. I figured I couldn't make the walls look worse. So I scraped off the loose stuff, washed it down, sanded a little, then got to it.

Usually I get bored doing stuff like that, and pretty soon get careless, splattering the paint or getting some on the porcelain or on the window. But that morning I was careful to get the right amount of paint on the roller and to spread it on the wall evenly. I even did the window slowly. When I finished it looked really good, and I thought how pleased Mom would be when she returned.

In the afternoon I took my bike out and rode the trail down to University Village in Seattle. Nobody else was out, so I really moved, breaking a sweat. It started drizzling on the way back, and the misty air felt tremendous.

When I reached the railroad trestle in Bothell I saw Michael Ushakov. He grinned at me and waved. I thought of Katya and felt guilty that I'd never gone over to see him, so I stopped. He came right up next to my bicycle and started fingering my light, repeatedly pushing the yellow button that turned it off and on.

"You didn't have this before, did you?"

It was like him to notice anything new.

"No," I said, "it was a Christmas gift."

"From your mom?"

"From my brother."

"Scott?"

"Yeah, Scott."

"Scott's over at my house a lot. I like Scott."

I smiled at that. He pushed the yellow button a few more times. There wasn't anything more to say. I slung my leg over the frame. "You should go home now, Michael," I said. "You're going to get drenched if you stay out."

"Okay," he said. "See ya."

As I pedaled off I looked over my shoulder. He was headed right back to the railroad trestle.

My grades had arrived in the mail. I stared at the envelope for a while, took a deep breath, then ripped into it. Two C+'s, three B's, and an A in P.E. It wouldn't make my mother happy, but I'd be eligible to play.

I stuck a frozen pizza into the oven. After I ate, I popped a Sonics tape into the VCR, one where Payton scored thirty points on Allen Iverson. It was a great game, but I didn't watch it closely. Mainly I listened for the gate to creak open.

The Sonics game ended and I started on an old Tom Hanks movie. Still no Trent. Then, around nine, there was a lot of commotion at the Dawson house. Mrs. Dawson came down the front porch steps, yelling at Zack. Zack screamed right back. The shouting went on for at least five minutes before the Corolla raced off, tires squealing.

That was that, I figured. No Trent. But a minute later I heard him on the court, and about ten seconds later I was headed out the back door. Once I stepped outside, I nodded to him. He nodded back, took a hard dribble, pulled up, missed a fifteen footer, and we were at it again.

I don't know how long we went one-on-one. An hour maybe, with neither of us talking at all. Then — out of nowhere — Trent stopped. "You block out really well on the boards. Never foul or anything."

"Thanks," I said, surprised. Then it hit me what he was after. "You want me to show you some tricks my dad taught me?"

He dribbled the ball a couple of times. "Yeah, sure."

So I broke down the moves for him, piece by piece. He was a quick learner, and within ten minutes he was blocking out better than I do. "That's good," I said. "Really good."

He took a little jump shot, swished it, then looked at me. "I passed."

"What?" I asked, not following.

"My classes. I passed everything. I'm eligible."

"That's great," I said, and I reached out and kind of shook his shoulder. "Way to go. You'll play a lot."

"Think so?"

"You bet. You bring that instant energy when you come in. You'll get minutes."

He took another jump shot, missed long, retrieved it.

"I've never played in a real game, with a scoreboard and real refs and all that stuff. I've never even had a uniform."

"Well, you'll get one now. Coach will have one ready for

you at the next practice. You wait and see."

We shot a couple of times each, then he spoke again. "Do you keep them at the end of the season?"

"Keep what?"

"The uniforms. Do you keep them?"

It was a good thing it was dark, because I had to smile at his question. He was like a kid at Christmas, all excited. "No," I said, making sure my voice was even. "They go back. As a matter of fact, if you don't get them washed and ironed, you pay a fine."

The following night we played again. It was the last night Mom and Scott would be away. All in all, I was glad they were coming back—the house was lonely without them—but Mom wouldn't let me play basketball late into the night, the way I'd been doing, and I was going to miss that freedom.

Something was wrong with Trent, though. He was edgy, fouling me more and scowling when I called him on it, acting a little like the Trent of old.

Around ten o'clock, right when we were going at it hard, the gate opened. I picked up my dribble and squinted into the darkness. "Who's there?"

Zack's voice rang out. "Come on, Trent, let's go."

I could hear Trent breathing in the still air. "Where?"

Zack's voice was commanding. "You know where. Now come on."

For a second, it was like being back at Canyon Park in the summer. Zack shows; Trent goes. Only this time Trent didn't go. "No. I'm playing basketball."

Zack took a couple of steps forward. He patted the pocket of his jacket. "I got them."

Trent dribbled the ball once, then held it. "I don't care. I'm playing basketball."

Zack came right onto the court. "You promised me."

Trent faced him down. "I promised nothing."

For a long moment there was silence. Then Zack was gone, out of the yard. Seconds later the Corolla roared off into the night.

"What was that all about?" I asked.

"Nothing," Trent snapped. He bricked a jumper off the front rim. "Let's just play."

He tried to get going, but his game was way off. Pretty soon he stopped entirely. "I've had enough," he mumbled.

"Come on," I said. "A little longer."

He shook his head, picked up his sweatshirt, and headed off the court. No liter of Pepsi, no talk.

Inside, I took a shower. Then I went down to the kitchen and made myself a peanut butter sandwich. I was sitting at the table, looking out into the night, when I heard the first siren. After that there were three more, each one screaming down 104th toward Main Street.

I slipped into the front room and looked across the street to the Dawson house. Nothing. Totally dark. But something kept me from going upstairs to bed. I sat down on the sofa by the window and waited.

I didn't have to wait long. Within ten minutes a police car roared up the street. The tires squealed as it came to a halt in front of the Dawson house. One officer popped out of the car and raced around to the back. The other one was up the walkway and onto the porch, his hand on his gun. Seconds later another police car pulled up behind the first.

I heard the knock all the way across the street—that's how loud it was. "Police! Open up!" For a while there was nothing, then the Dawson's front door opened and Ericka Dawson stepped onto the porch, pulling the door closed behind her. She talked to the policeman for a moment. He showed her something, then she stepped aside as he crossed the threshold into her house.

The house had been dark, but within minutes every light was on. After what seemed like forever the policeman came out, alone. A little while later the first police car drove off. The motor on the second turned over, but instead of driving off, the car inched a hundred yards or so up the block, then came to a stop in a dark spot between streetlights. It was still sitting there an hour later when I finally went to bed.

Chapter 10 Early the next morning Scott and Mom returned. She'd bought some San Francisco sourdough bread at the airport, and we went into the kitchen and talked and ate. Scott unrolled a poster of whales from the Monterey aquarium, and he showed off the third-place medal he'd won at the jazz competition. "We got called back for two encores. It was awesome."

"That's great," I said. "Congratulations."

Then Mom started. She described the auditoriums, the

audiences, the cheering. "Everywhere you turned there was music. The whole city was alive with it. Oh, I wish you could have been there!"

They ran out of things to say just about when the bread was gone. There was a stretch of silence, then Scott stood. "I'm going to call Katya."

"Scott, you spent every minute on the trip with her. Give the girl some room to breathe."

"I told her I'd call. I can't not do it."

Mom frowned, then took her suitcase to her bedroom. I wandered out to the front room, dropped onto the sofa, pulled the curtains back a bit, and peeked out across the street. The police car was gone, but in its place was another car I'd never seen on our block, a large, dark Chevy. A man was sitting inside reading a newspaper.

A moment later Scott came downstairs. "That was quick," Mom said, coming out of her bedroom.

"She wasn't home," Scott replied, worried.

"So she went someplace," Mom replied. "She doesn't have to ask your permission, does she?"

"But we were going into Seattle today. To Gameworks."

"Give her a few minutes and call again. Only I'm warning you. You'll suffocate her if you don't give her some privacy."

Scott went upstairs as Mom sat down in the chair across from me. "How about you? What did you do with yourself while we were gone, besides paint the bathroom? It looks great by the way. Thank you."

"Nothing much. I watched some TV, read a little, shot some hoops."

"Did your father come by?"

I hadn't thought about him at all. "No, he didn't."

She didn't say anything, but I could tell she was angry. I stood. "I'll be in the back," I said.

"That basketball court has turned out to be a pretty good thing for you, hasn't it?"

"Yeah, it has."

I shot hoops for an hour or so. When I came back inside, the big Chevy was still parked up the block, and Scott was still moping around. "Has the newspaper come?" I asked him.

"Yeah. Mom brought it in. It's on the table."

Mom laughs at the *Eastside Journal*. She says that if a bomb exploded in their own office, the *Seattle Times* would have the story first. She subscribes only because I read the sports section cover-to-cover.

I pulled off the rubber band. The paper unrolled in front of me. I'd intended to go right to the sports pages to see if they had the scores from the Victoria tournament, but the head-line jumped out at me. BOTHELL YOUTH SHOT ON TRAIL. Quickly my eyes raced through the paragraphs. "Mom," I said as I read. "Scott. Come here."

There must have been something in my voice that drew them, because they both came immediately.

"What is it?" my mother said. "What's happened?"

I pointed to the headline. "It's Michael Ushakov. He's been shot."

Part
Four

Chapter 1

It was as if an earthquake had rocked our house — everybody was reeling. Mom grabbed the newspaper from me, put a hand to her mouth, then dropped it, saying, "Oh my God."

Scott went straight to the phone.

"Don't bother," Mom said. "I'm sure she's at the hospital." Mom turned to me. "Does it say where they took him?"

I snatched the newspaper from the ground. "Yeah, here it is. University Hospital."

"We can be there in half an hour. Poor Mrs. Ushakov."

Scott grabbed his coat. Mom looked around for her purse for a moment, found it, then turned to me. "Are you coming?"

I shook my head. "I'd just be in the way."

She didn't argue. "All right, but you're on your own. I don't know when we'll be back."

A minute later she and Scott were gone. I stayed inside for maybe ten minutes, working up my courage. Then I opened the front door and walked out to the strange car. The man

129

inside was reading the newspaper. I tapped on the window. "Are you a policeman?" I asked when he rolled it down.

"What do you want, kid?"

"I think I know something about what happened last night."

He put the newspaper on the seat next to him and motioned toward my house. "You live there?"

"Yeah."

He pulled out his wallet, showed me his identification. "I'm Officer Tomlinson. How about if I come in and we talk?"

I thought I knew so much, but I was finished in a couple of minutes. "Let me see if I've got this right," he said, looking over his notes. "You were playing basketball with Trent Dawson last night. Around ten, Zack Dawson came up. He seemed to have gotten hold of something, something Trent knew about. They argued a little, and then Zack left. Is that it?"

I nodded.

"But you didn't see what he had inside his coat?"

"No."

He tapped his pencil against his note pad. "How long did Trent stay with you once Zack had left?"

I felt my chest tighten. "A while."

"How long is 'a while'? Two minutes...thirty...an hour?"

"At least ten minutes," I said. Then I added: "Probably more like twenty."

He closed his notebook.

I screwed up my courage. "Was it Zack? Did he shoot Michael?"

"I can't answer that," he said, standing. "But we'd sure like to talk to him. In fact, we'd like to talk with both Dawson boys. So if you see either of them, or they get in touch with you, you tell them that. And then you call us right away. You understand? Right away."

He left, and not more than a minute later the telephone rang. I raced to pick it up, thinking it was Mom, but it was Luke. Earlier in the day I'd been hoping he'd call, but now the basketball team seemed as if it were part of a world I'd left.

To him it was everything. I asked how Victoria had been, and his voice bubbled with excitement. "Great. We had tea at this huge old hotel, the Empress. I know it sounds stupid, but it was fun, like being in England. And there's this Miniature World where all the big battles from the two world wars are set up. There's another place called..." He rattled on and on, with me saying "Yeah" or "Sounds great" every thirty seconds or so. Finally he stopped.

"How'd you do in the tournament?" I asked.

He groaned. "We lost all three games. None was even close. We were totally squashed." He paused. "That's the bad news. The good news — for you — is how we lost. Fabroa got himself in foul trouble every game. And Chang just isn't quick enough to play point guard. The first night he got double-teamed and couldn't handle it. After that every team doubled him as soon as he touched the ball. Turnovers, fouls, sloppy defense. You name it; we did it. O'Leary was going absolutely crazy on the bench."

"That's too bad," I said.

"Yeah, yeah. For the team. But not for you. With a couple

of good practices, you'll be starting Thursday against Lake Washington." He paused, waiting for me to show some excitement. When I didn't, he noticed. "Something wrong, Nick?"

I should've told him about Michael Ushakov, but I couldn't bring myself to, maybe because I kept hoping that somehow it would all go away. "No," I said. "Nothing's wrong."

Chapter 2 Mom came home at six carrying a bag of groceries. "Michael lost a lot of blood," she said as she set the bag on the kitchen table and began unpacking it. "They took a bullet out of his chest, three inches from his heart. But he's going to make it." Her voice caught, and she stopped to blow her nose. Then she was all business again. "I'm going to make some spaghetti and bring it over to the Ushakovs. I'm sure they haven't had a decent meal all day. Scott's over there now with Katya. He'll probably stay and eat with them. You and I can get something later. Okay?"

"Sure," I said. Then, as she turned on the burner under the big pot of water, I asked the question I'd been afraid to ask. "Do they know who did it?"

She nodded in the direction of the Dawson house, her eyes filling with tears. "It was Zack," she whispered. Then she cut open the package of spaghetti and broke the long strands in half. Watching her fight back tears made my eyes well up. If I'd stayed there I'd have been bawling like a baby, so I went up to my room and turned on the radio.

Mom brought the spaghetti over to the Ushakovs and then

phoned to say she wouldn't be home until late. I ended up eating a ham sandwich alone at the kitchen table. Afterwards I tried to watch television, but I couldn't get interested. Around eight the telephone rang again. This time Dad's voice was on the other end of the line.

He started out by grilling me about what had happened. After I'd told him everything I knew, there was a long pause. Then came the lecture. If I saw Zack, I was to call the police. "But don't give your name. Just say where he is and then hang up. You understand?"

"Dad, there's a police car parked in front of his house. They don't need me looking for him. If he comes around here, they'll see him."

"You don't know that." His voice was sharp. "Now do you understand what I'm saying?"

"Yeah, I understand."

"Good. And from now on, as far as you're concerned Trent Dawson doesn't exist. You see him, you treat him like he's a ghost. I don't want you to have anything to do with him. Not play basketball with him, not talk to him, not even nod hello to him. Stay completely clear."

"But Trent didn't do anything," I said. "He was with me when it happened."

"I don't care if he was with the president of the United States. You're to have nothing to do with him. Am I making myself clear?"

"Yeah," I muttered.

"Okay then. That's settled." There was a long pause. "Is your mom there?"

"No, she and Scott are at the Ushakovs."

"Well, you tell her I called. And you tell Scott what I said about both Dawsons, because the same things go for him."

"Okay."

Again there was a long pause. Then he took me by surprise. "I love you, Son," he said. "I don't mean to yell at you. I just want you to be safe."

"I love you too, Dad," I said.

After I hung up the phone, I sat on the sofa and stared at the design in the carpet, that big lump back in my throat. Then, out of nowhere, I got mad. If he loved me so damn much, why did I only hear from him when he wanted to give me orders or criticize what I was doing?

Chapter 3

I went downstairs, turned on the television, and watched half an hour of some college game on ESPN. I couldn't tell you what the score was or which teams were playing. I had too much nervous energy to stay still, so I flicked the TV off, climbed upstairs to my room, dug my basketball from the closet, and went outside to shoot around.

The evening was cold and damp. The mist was so heavy you could see it against the streetlights. I'd shot around for ten minutes or so when I clanged a jumper off the back iron and the ball bounded off the court. As I moved to retrieve it I spotted something back in the deepest corner of our yard — a shape huddled under a little overhang that jutted out from the shed.

"Is somebody there?" I called, holding the ball against my hip. There was no answer, but I noticed the slightest movement. "Who's there?"

Trent stepped out of the darkness. "It's me."

His face was gray, his hair matted down by the rain. But it was his eyes that had changed most. They'd always been alive—sometimes crazy-alive, but always alive. Now they looked dead.

"What's up?" I said.

"I don't know, Nick," he answered. "You tell me."

I knew what he was after. "My mom was at the hospital. Michael is going to be okay. He's not going to die or anything."

I could see him breathing, long deep breaths of relief, the gray-white vapor showing against the darkness of the night. One deep breath and then another.

"Trent," I said, "what happened?"

Another long pause, and then his voice: "It's crazy. We've had the gun for years, hidden away in a closet. We always talked about going down to the trail some night and shooting into the water, or at a tree or something, but we never had any bullets. That's what Zack was showing me last night— that he'd gotten bullets. When I wouldn't go with him, he went down there alone. Michael was standing on the bridge, the way he does, and Zack just sort of waved the gun at him and pulled the trigger. That was the first time he'd ever fired it. The first time. He didn't think it worked. He didn't mean to hurt anybody. It was a fluke, an accident."

I made myself say the words. "He's got to turn himself in."

Trent's eyes narrowed. "No way! He's eighteen now. You understand what that means? They'll put him in prison. Not juvenile hall. Prison. With real criminals. He could get killed in there."

"They won't if he explains what happened."

"Are you kidding? Nobody would believe him. Our only chance is to get away, to get someplace far away where nobody knows us."

My body tensed. "What do you mean *us?* You're not going with him, are you?"

He looked away. "I've got to. He's my brother."

The wind had come up and a hard rain had started to fall. I shuddered from the cold. Trent had to be frozen to the bone, too. "Look," I said, "come inside with me. No one's home. You can sleep downstairs on the sofa, think things over tonight, then decide tomorrow."

He shook his head. "I can't. I've got to meet Zack, tell him Michael's going to be all right. He thinks he killed him."

"So tell him. Then come back here. Okay?"

He turned and headed back into the darkness.

"Okay?" I called again, but he didn't answer.

I returned inside. I remembered what Officer Tomlinson had said, what my dad had said, and my eyes were drawn to the telephone. But instead of phoning, I took a long shower. Then I dressed, went downstairs, and wandered around the house, looking out the windows, listening.

If I hadn't been listening, I wouldn't have heard it. That's how soft the knock was. But I did hear it, and when I opened the back door, Trent was there.

136

"You hungry?" I asked, once he'd come in.

He nodded. "Yeah, I guess."

I motioned to the kitchen table. "Sit down. I'll make you something."

After I'd gone into the front room and cranked up the thermostat, I made him a peanut butter sandwich. While he was eating, I boiled water in the microwave, dumped a couple of tablespoons of Nestlés Quik into a cup, and poured the water into it. The heat duct was filling the kitchen with warm air as I handed the steaming drink to Trent. He held it in two hands, his shoulders hunched, and sipped greedily, drinking as if he'd been rescued from the ocean.

When he finished, I led him downstairs and gave him some blankets. "Nobody will bother you," I said. "I'll wake you early tomorrow morning, and then you can do whatever you want." He nodded, his eyes glazed with exhaustion.

Mom and Scott were certain to come home soon, and when they did, I had to make sure they didn't go downstairs. So I plunked myself down in the chair by the front door and waited. I found myself falling asleep and then jerking back awake.

Twelve-thirteen... Twelve forty-seven... One o'clock.

Finally, at one-thirty, the front door opened and my mother and Scott stepped inside. My mother was startled to see me. "What are you doing up?"

I was so tired I could hardly think. "I couldn't sleep," I managed. "I wanted to hear, you know..." My voice trailed off.

"Michael has developed a blood clot in his leg," Mom said.

"It happens sometimes, in cases like his. They're going to operate tomorrow. If all goes well, he'll be out of the hospital within a week."

Scott brushed by me, yawning. "I'm going to bed."

"You look tired too," I said to Mom. "You should go to bed."

Suspicion came to her eyes. "Nick, what's going on? Has something else happened?"

"No. I just couldn't sleep with you and Scott gone."

She stared at me. I forced myself to meet her eyes. "All right. We're home now. It's time for all of us to go to bed. This has been a long, long day."

It was a long night, too. I suppose I slept some of it, but I was awake more than I was asleep. At five in the morning I headed downstairs. At the bottom stair, I stopped. "Trent," I whispered into the darkness, "you awake?"

"Yeah," came the reply.

A few minutes later we were both in the kitchen. I stuck some English muffins in the toaster oven and found some vanilla yogurt in the refrigerator. He ate everything I put in front of him, then pulled his coat around him and stood.

"What now?" I asked.

He shrugged. "Home, I guess. Sleep some more, and then talk to the police, get that over with. After that, I wait."

"For what?"

"For Zack. He took off last night. Once he gets set up somewhere, he's going to send word."

"And you're going to go?"

"I told you. He's my brother."

Chapter 4 That night Katya came over for dinner. It was a celebration of sorts. The operation to remove the blood clot had been a success. Michael was going to be fine. "He looks better already," Katya said. "His skin has color again, and he was talking the way he normally does."

After dinner the conversation turned to Zack. They were all sure he'd get caught. Scott said he should get ten years in jail, minimum. My mother thought sending him to jail would make him more of a criminal when he came out. "Then keep him in jail," Katya declared. "Keep him there his whole life."

"What do you think?" Scott said, turning to me.

"To tell you the truth," I stammered, "I've been thinking about Trent and what's going to happen with him."

"Why do you care?" Katya asked.

"I don't know," I said. "He's in my classes, on my..."

"Basketball team?" she said, finishing my sentence for me, her voice filled with scorn. "His brother almost kills Michael, and all you're worried about is your basketball team."

"That's not true," I said. "I care about Michael."

Her eyes flashed. "Then why haven't you been to see him? Tell me that? You haven't been to the hospital once. You haven't even called."

All three were staring at me now. I felt like a bug under a microscope. "I didn't want to be in the way," I managed.

Katya tossed her head back and laughed scornfully. "Oh, right. Michael has had *so* many visitors. His thousands of friends have just filled the hospital. They set up a number system, like—"

My mother interrupted. "That's enough, Katya."

Katya didn't stop. "I'm sorry, Mrs. Abbott, but he—"

"You've made your point, Katya."

"I'll visit Michael tomorrow," I said. "I promise."

"Don't bother," Katya snapped.

Chapter 5 In the hallways before school on Monday, the conversations were all about the shooting. I didn't want to hear them, so I went straight to my first-period class. As I entered the room, I looked to the back row in the corner where Trent normally sat. The chair was empty.

I took my normal spot, opened a book, and pretended to read. The room slowly filled. When about half the class was there, Martha Judkins—a girl I wish I knew better—started railing against Zack. She sounded exactly like Katya, saying how she thought Zack should spend the rest of his life in jail.

I listened for as long as I could, then spoke up. "You don't really know what happened, Martha. Nobody does. Maybe the whole thing was an accident."

She looked at me as if I'd grown a second head. "Oh, sure, Nick. Zack Dawson just *happens* to shoot the guy who *happened* to turn him in for killing those geese or chickens or whatever they were. What's the chance of that?"

Kids around me snickered. I felt stupid, stupid and childish, and I was glad when class started.

Somehow I made it through the morning. When lunchtime rolled around, out of habit I started toward the cafeteria. But then I stopped myself. I wasn't that hungry, and I couldn't bear to sit at a table and listen to kids around me talk about Zack, or Michael, or Trent.

From a vending machine I bought peanut butter crackers, some cookies, and a Coke, then headed outside. There are some huge fir trees at one corner of the Bothell High campus. I hunched up under one of them, sheltered a little from the January cold and wind, and ate.

I didn't want to think about anything, but there was no escaping what had happened. The whole scene played itself out in my mind. Michael walking over the wooden footbridge at Bothell Landing, singing some stupid song probably; Zack on the wooded side of the bridge, half hidden in the trees that line the trail, watching Michael come toward him, seeing him silhouetted against the light.

That's when it got really hard.

Because Martha was right. How can someone accidentally raise a gun, accidentally point it at someone, and accidentally fire? How can someone hear the shot, feel the recoil of the gun, watch a person fall, and then run? Zack must have known he wasn't playing a game, not once the gun went off and Michael went down. He must have known that the whole thing had turned real, had always been real. How could he leave Michael lying on that bridge bleeding his life away?

I was actually glad when it was time to head back to class, though once I was in the building the day dragged again. When the final bell rang, I felt like going home, but I knew if I skipped practice O'Leary would suspend me, and maybe even boot me off the team.

In the locker room guys were mulling over the Victoria trip and how badly they'd played. Fabroa went on and on about some foul in the fourth quarter that he swore he hadn't committed. "You were robbed," McShane agreed, nodding. "Those were the worst refs ever."

As they droned on I grew angry. Trent was on the team. Didn't anybody notice that he wasn't there? Didn't any of them wonder what was happening to him? I thought O'Leary would say something, but he didn't. We went straight into our drills, all business.

I turned off my mind and let my body take over. At the other practices I'd been keeping a box score in my mind. How many points did I have? Assists? Turnovers? How many did Fabroa have? Chang? Did O'Leary see that good play? Did he miss that bad one?

That practice I didn't worry about Fabroa's game or Chang's. I didn't worry about scoring or making assists or what O'Leary saw or didn't see. I took my shot when I was open, passed when I wasn't, hustled back on defense, and watched for opportunities.

O'Leary blew his whistle. "That's it. Everybody over here!" I looked at the clock, stunned. I couldn't believe that two hours had passed.

I shuffled over to O'Leary, who gave us a pep talk about how our important league games were still coming up, how we could turn the season around if we dedicated ourselves to winning. "So let's do it!" he said, and the guys let out a cheer.

That day, for the first time in a long time, I walked home with Luke. For block after block he talked basketball, mostly about my game: how well I'd played in practice, how the team needed a leader on the court, how if I played like that all the time, we really could put together a winning streak. "You're the key to the whole season."

We'd reached the place where he split off to go to his home in the Highlands. "Don't you think it's weird Coach didn't say anything about Trent?" I asked. "You'd think he'd say *something*, wouldn't you?"

Luke looked off. "What's there to say? You had the guy pegged. He's trouble. We're better off without him."

"And that's it? End of story?"

"You think anybody would sweat it if I got myself in trouble?" Luke snapped. "Because I don't. They'd just say: *Oh yeah, those black guys. What do you expect?* Trent's had his chances. I'm not spending my life worrying about him."

Dinner was ready as soon as I walked in the door. Scott was going with the Ushakovs to University Hospital. It was going to be Michael's last night there. "You should go, too," Mom said to me.

"I will," I answered, and then I looked at Scott. "Unless you don't think Katya wants me."

"Of course she wants you. And Michael does, too."

The Ushakovs were late. As I sat with Scott in the front room waiting, I tried to feel good about going to see Michael, but instead I kept thinking about Trent. Me, Scott, Katya, Luke, Michael Ushakov—we all had someone holding onto us, someone watching out for us. Only Trent had nobody and nothing.

I hustled upstairs, grabbed the basketball out of my closet, then headed downstairs. I plopped down in the chair across from Scott and started to lace up my basketball shoes. I knew what I had to do.

"The Ushakovs will be here any minute," Scott said, perplexed.

"I'm not going to the hospital," I answered.

"What are you talking about? You just said you were."

"Well, I'm not."

"So where are you going?"

"I'm going to play basketball with Trent, if he'll play."

Scott's eyes bugged out. "You're going to shoot hoops with Trent while Michael's lying in the hospital? You've got to be kidding."

Just then Mom entered the room. Immediately she spotted the basketball on the sofa. "What's the ball for?"

"That's what I asked him," Scott said. "Wait until you hear his answer."

She looked at me.

"I'm not going to the hospital, Mom. I'm going to shoot hoops with Trent."

She put her hands on her hips. "No, you're not, young man. You're going to the hospital to visit Michael, just as you said you would, and as you should have done the very first day. And you're going to have absolutely nothing to do with Trent Dawson."

I forced myself to stay calm. "Everybody seems to be forgetting something. Trent didn't go with Zack that night. He stayed with me. Do you understand? He stayed with me."

She stepped back a little. There was a long pause. "And I'm glad he did, Nick. I'm very glad he did. But just because you helped him once doesn't mean you have to do it all the time. And it certainly doesn't mean you have to go over there now, with Michael still in the hospital."

I took a deep breath. "There will be a bunch of people with Michael. Trent's got nobody."

Scott groaned. "Katya was right about you. She had you —"

"Scott, be still!" Mom commanded. Our eyes met. I could feel her thinking. Ten seconds ticked by. Then ten more. "Go," she said at last.

"Are you crazy?" Scott raged. "What's Dad going to say?"

Quickly, before she could change her mind, I opened the front door and stepped into the night.

Chapter 6 I gave Trent's front door a good firm rap. For a long time there was no response. Then a light went on, and I heard footsteps on the stairs. The door opened. He didn't say anything; he just looked. I held the basketball in front of me. "You want to shoot some?"

His head tilted suspiciously. "What's this all about?"

"It's not about anything," I replied. "Just hoops."

He looked at me for what seemed like forever, then shrugged. "Sure, why not?"

We played late into the night, one-on-one basketball, hard

to the hoop, no harm—no foul. We didn't stop until Mr. Shubert, who lives in the house behind us, opened his sliding porch door and yelled: "Guys, it's late. Give it a rest."

Trent came inside with me and sat at the kitchen table. I got a liter of Pepsi from the refrigerator and two glasses from the cupboard. "We had a pretty good practice today," I said, slipping into the chair across from him. "You going to be there tomorrow?"

He laughed. "What do you think? You think they want me back at school, back at practice?"

I poured the Pepsi into the glasses. "Since when did Trent Dawson ever care what other people want or think?"

He shot me a look. "I don't care."

I ate a handful of peanuts from a bowl on the kitchen table. "So surprise everybody. Go to school tomorrow. Go to practice. Later on you could come here if you want. We could knock off our homework, then shoot around just the way we did over Christmas."

A mocking smile came to his lips. "You know, I've talked to a few counselors over the years. More than a few, in fact. I know this little game you're playing. I know it inside and out."

"There's no game," I insisted. "You can't just sit in your house waiting for Zack to call. It could be months, right? You'll die of boredom. So why not play basketball until he does?"

He sat back in his chair and looked at me, trying to make me look away. But I didn't. I kept my eyes right on his. At last he picked up his Pepsi and drank until it was gone.

"Okay," he said, standing. "Until I hear from Zack, I'll go to your school and I'll play on your basketball team and I'll shoot around with you at night. But I'm doing this for me—not for you or anybody else—and I'm doing it for as long as I want, and not a second longer. You got it?"

I swallowed. "Yeah, I got it."

He nodded, and then he was out the door.

Chapter 7 The next morning Trent was sitting at the bottom of his porch steps, his backpack by his side. I didn't know if he was waiting for me or for something else, or if he was just sitting there. Then his eye caught mine, and he stood, picking his backpack up as he did. I crossed the street. "How's it going?" I asked.

"Not bad."

I looked down the sidewalk, dotted with kids headed to Bothell High. "You want to get moving?"

"Yeah, I guess."

Until that day, I'd always felt at home on that walk. But that morning—with Trent at my side—kids who normally would have crossed the street and walked in with me, totally ignored me. In the hallways at school it was more of the same. Faces would light up, then they'd spot Trent, and suddenly I was invisible. They'd wanted him to go away; they'd thought he was gone; and I'd brought him back.

The locker room was just like school. Nobody said anything outright. It was all: "Hey, Trent, how's it going? Hey,

Nick, what's up?" Coach O'Leary came in and gave Trent a smile and a handshake. But even in his eyes I could see the suspicion.

On the court O'Leary called us to him and gave the same talk he always gave before practice. Still I didn't relax. I felt as if I were sitting behind home plate at a Mariners game, but that my ticket was no good and I knew it, and that at any second I'd feel fingers digging into my shoulder and hear a voice telling me to get out.

Trent and I were both third stringers, so we didn't start the scrimmage. But once O'Leary stuck us in, we made sure he didn't yank us out. Inside the lines, going all out, I didn't have to think. My mind turned off and my body took over. On defense I was up in Fabroa's face, playing him so tight he didn't even want the ball. Trent patrolled the key, muscling guys out of the way, grabbing rebounds.

We ran the fast break every chance we got. Sometimes I'd take the ball all the way; sometimes I'd thread the needle with a bounce pass that Trent would take to the basket for two points. The other second-teamers were just filling up space. It was really the two of us against the entire first team, and we were like a fireball scorching everything in its path. Just before practice ended, I actually bounced a pass to Trent that went between Luke's legs. Trent laid the ball in for an easy score, and Luke's face reddened. After practice all the starters showered and left quickly, their shoulders slumped just as though they'd lost a real game.

Trent and I walked home together. "You played great," I told him. "You were tremendous."

He smiled then, almost in spite of himself. "I did okay."

"You did more than okay. You ate their lunch."

"You weren't so bad yourself."

I wanted to keep talking about practice, but I couldn't keep him going. By the time we reached our block we were walking in silence. "We're done with dinner around seven," I said then. "If you want, you can come over. We could do our math, then shoot around. That sound okay?"

I expected him to turn me down, but he shrugged. "Yeah, sure. Why not?"

Chapter 8

Thursday night we took on the Franklin Earthquake in their gym. At the team meeting after school, Coach O'Leary had us sit on the bleachers while he gave out the standard information: game time, address of the school, maps for anybody who needed one.

Once the details were taken care of, he paced back and forth. You could hear him breathing through his nose like a mad bull about to charge. Finally, he lit into us. "We're two and five this year, a lousy record. But we're not a lousy team. Or at least I don't think we are. These Franklin kids think they're going to run over us. They think we're nothing." He stopped and surveyed us, catching each guy's eye in turn. Some looked away; some didn't. I didn't. "Tonight is gut-check time. Tonight we'll see what you've got."

Mom had agreed to give Trent a ride to the game. When Scott heard that at dinner, he got furious. "Why don't you have the guy move in with us? He studies in our kitchen, eats the food out of our refrigerator, shoots hoops in the yard. Now we taxi him around. The only thing left is to get him a bed."

"What are you getting riled up about?" I said. "It's just a ride."

"It's not just a ride and you know it. I live here too, you know. Katya won't come around if Trent's here all the time. And I'll tell you something else. He knows where Zack is — and his mom does too. I'll bet you anything they're sending him money, helping him. It's not right, and it's not right for us to do anything that helps them."

His speech over, he stood, threw his napkin down, and left the table. "Where are you going?" Mom asked.

"I'm going to phone Katya. I'll get a ride from her. I'm not getting in the car with Trent."

Mom and I finished dinner in silence. We could hear Scott make his phone call, hear his voice cheer as he got the answer he wanted. When he went upstairs, Mom asked if there was some other way Trent could get to the next game. I shook my head. "And the basketball in our yard every night? And the studying at the kitchen table? There's no other place he could go?"

"I'm the only friend he's got."

She put her elbows on the table, rested her chin on her hands. "But you're not the only son I have."

"Come on, Mom," I pleaded. "Riding with Katya is hardly some ordeal for Scott."

"I'm not talking about that. I'm talking about the other

things. You don't really know how deeply involved Trent is in all of this, do you?"

"He's not a bad guy, Mom. I know that."

"That's not the question. The question is whether he's done bad things."

She wasn't happy about driving Trent, but she was true to her word. She even made small talk with him in the car, telling him how great it was that he'd raised his grades so that he could play: the school-is-more-important-than-sports routine. He barely answered. Instead he kept unzipping his bag, rooting around in there to make sure he had all his stuff, then zipping it closed.

We were the last to arrive. I had to drag myself up the long stairway to the gym, but Trent took the stairs two at a time. Inside the locker room I nodded to Luke, to Carver, to the other guys, and they nodded back. But there was a wall between Trent and me and the rest of the team.

O'Leary called us to a chalkboard by the door. He put the names of the starters up, and underneath he listed Brian Chang's name. Below them, in a group of four, were the other second-stringers. Neither Trent's name nor my name was on the board at all.

"Listen up," he said, clapping his hands for attention.

"This place is a snake pit. It's going to be crazy out there. Brian, you be ready. You're first off the bench. You four"—he tapped the second group of names with his chalk—"you'll rotate in toward the end of the first quarter. And if you don't see your name up here"—this was for Trent and me—"don't think that means you aren't playing. I'll use you anytime I need you, so keep your head in the game. Now let's go!"

As I took the court, it was as if I was carrying around a whole suitcase of stuff weighing me down. I was mad about the way the guys froze me out, froze Trent out, mad about being blamed for the early losses, mad about being benched by O'Leary, mad about being left behind when the team went to Victoria, mad about my dad not coming to the game. My name being left off the blackboard was one more thing to stuff in that suitcase.

I was sluggish all through warm-ups. I never looked for my mom, never even glanced at the Franklin guys. It wasn't until the horn sounded and we headed to the bench that I even noticed Trent.

He was trying to be stone-faced. His mouth was straight, his jaw tight, but his eyes—his eyes were glowing. You'd have thought he was starting the game, instead of being buried at the end of the bench.

I couldn't figure it. Then, as the band played the "Star Spangled Banner," I remembered the questions he'd asked about the uniform, the way he kept checking his bag in the car, and suddenly I understood. This was his first real game. He was somewhere he never thought he'd be, doing something he never thought he'd do.

O'Leary was right about Franklin—they didn't take us seriously. You could see it in the sloppy way they opened the game. Their guards were lightning quick, but instead of letting their natural ability have its way, they tried too much, forcing passes into tight spaces, looking to make the highlight reel.

But it wasn't just the guards. Their star, a tall muscular black kid named Robby Wilkes, was doing dipsy-doodle stuff instead of taking the ball strong to the hole. A couple of spinning jumpers actually went down for him, which encouraged him to try even more circus shots.

Because of Franklin's sloppy play, we hung close through the first quarter. When Fabroa needed a breather, Chang got the call. Those Franklin guys could have eaten him alive if they'd pressed. But they played soft, and when he's not pressured, Chang does okay. He actually nailed a three-pointer at the buzzer that put us up 12–11.

The Earthquake's coach must have given his team an earful during the break because they came out charged for the second quarter. On their first possession Wilkes powered straight to the hoop—nothing fancy—for a driving dunk. Immediately they slapped on a full-court, trapping press.

Their press had energy, but I could see how to beat it. Their guards were quick, but other than Robby Wilkes, the front-line players were plodders. All Fabroa had to do was wait for the trap to come, then make one good pass over the top to Markey or Carver or Luke, and we would have been off for the lay-in or the short jumper. But time after time Fabroa tried to make his pass before the double-team reached him, and those passes would get picked off. Then it was the Earthquakes racing to the basket, with us watching.

Quickly they pulled out to an eight-point lead. O'Leary

called time-out. He looked at Chang and then at me. I'm faster, and what we needed was speed. But it was Chang who got the nod.

Fresh legs matter. For a couple of minutes he did better than Fabroa. But with three minutes left in the half, Franklin changed tactics. Instead of a trapping, zone press, they went man-to-man. They had their fastest guard hound Chang the length of the court, using the other guys to fill the passing lanes. Chang couldn't break the one-on-one pressure, couldn't make the pass. On four straight possessions he turned the ball over. Franklin's gym was rocking, and O'Leary's time out did nothing to slow the momentum. At the half we were down 37–19.

O'Leary railed at us in the locker room, but when you haven't played, it's hard to listen. Back on the bench at the start of the second half, I found myself hoping we'd fall even farther behind. Thirty points down and I figured O'Leary would stick both Trent and me in.

But Franklin took off the press at the start of the third quarter, and their intensity came off, too. We didn't cut into their lead, but they didn't extend it. At least not for most of the quarter. Then Fabroa sat down and Chang came in for the last two minutes of the third quarter. He immediately threw away a couple of passes and made a stupid foul. The quarter ended with Franklin making a 9–2 run that stretched their lead to twenty-five. O'Leary turned sideways in his seat, a scowl on his face, and looked at Trent and me. "Abbott... Dawson, you're starting the fourth quarter."

The game was over. Carver was on the bench; Luke was

on the bench. There were more people eating hot dogs out in the lobby than there were up in the stands, but Trent didn't care. It was the "Star Spangled Banner" all over again. He was in a game, in a *real* game, and his eyes were shining. And if it was good enough for him, then it was good enough for me.

Trent was so pumped up that for the first couple of minutes he was wild, bouncing around like a pinball, totally disrupting Franklin on one possession but then giving up an easy basket on the next. When the ref whistled him for a charging foul his fists clenched, but then he turned and raced downcourt, and I breathed easier. His first shot — a little jumper from the free-throw line I set up with penetration — was halfway done before it rattled out. Still, he drew the foul. He must have bounced the ball twenty times before he took the foul shot. It was a bullet, bricking off the back rim with so much force that the Franklin guys smiled. I sidled over to him. "Just like in my back yard," I whispered. He nodded, and his next shot was perfect.

With four minutes left he hit his stride and I hit mine. For the rest of the game we dominated that court. He'd haul down a rebound, give me a quick outlet pass, then fill a fast-break lane. I'd dance a pass through the defender's arms back to him for a driving lay-in, or I'd pull up and stick the jumper myself.

It was garbage time, and with their big lead the Franklin defenders weren't exactly up in our faces. Still, by the final buzzer we'd cut the twenty-five-point lead to twelve — and that's good playing at any time. As we walked off the court I saw the Franklin coach staring at Trent and me, wondering what would have happened had we played earlier. I hoped O'Leary was wondering the same thing.

In the car on the way home, Trent didn't exactly rattle on nonstop, but when I mentioned a shot or a rebound, he'd talk about it a little, and he couldn't keep that crooked smile from his face. "You were wonderful," Mom said to him. "Simply wonderful."

When Mom pulled onto our block, her headlights played on Trent's house. There were three cars and two motorcycles in the driveway, and more cars parked in front. Every light in the house was on. I looked at Trent; his face was tight.

"You want to come in for a little while?" I asked.

"That's okay."

"You sure?" I said, rubbing my hands together against the cold. "We could play some cards or something."

He shook his head. "No."

"See you tomorrow then."

"Yeah. See you."

I went inside, talked to Mom a little, then sat on the sofa by the window and stared across the street at Trent's house. Every once in a while his front door would open and somebody would spill out, laughing or swearing—or both. Our windows would rattle from the volume of the stereo until the door slammed shut again. The party was still going strong when I headed upstairs to my bedroom.

Chapter 9 The next evening Dad phoned. It seemed like forever since I'd talked with him, but it had only been a week since Michael Ushakov had been shot. "I'm flipping through tonight's newspaper," he said, his voice excited, "and whose name jumps off the page and smacks me in the face. Six points, four assists, two steals, and no turnovers. I told you to call me if you were going to play."

I laughed. "I didn't know I was going to."

"Well, how about against Roosevelt? That idiot coach isn't going to stick you back on the bench again, is he?"

"I'm not starting," I answered, "but at practice today I did get moved to second team. I should see some real minutes."

"I'll be there, and that's a promise." He paused, and his voice became serious. "I knew you could make it, Nick. I always believed in you."

When I hung up, I was smiling ear-to-ear. Then I turned and saw Scott. "Was that Dad?"

"Yeah."

"I knew he'd call once he saw your name in the paper."

"What's that supposed to mean?"

"You know what it means."

"No, I don't," I said.

He laughed mockingly as he pushed past me. "Fine, Nick. Have it your way."

It was different sitting on the bench during the first quarter of the Roosevelt game. I tried to stay cool and calm, but it was hard. O'Leary wasn't going to mess around; I was sure of it.

If the first-stringers fell behind, Trent and I were going in.

And fall behind they did. The Roughriders' point guard buried a three-pointer on his first shot, made a pull-up fifteen-foot jumper on his second, and then was perfect with another three-pointer a minute later. The last shot was unreal. Fabroa had his hand in the guy's face, but it was still dead center. We were down 11–2 when O'Leary popped off the bench.

"Nick, Trent!"

It's different going into a game in the first quarter rather than the fourth. *No need to rush,* I told myself as I stepped on the court. *Slow and easy.* Roosevelt couldn't keep up their hot shooting. No team could, not even an NBA team. All we had to do was play our game and we'd reel them in.

Sure enough, they went into a little funk. The guy I was guarding, who hadn't missed with Fabroa hanging all over him, suddenly couldn't sink anything, even when he juked me and was wide open from ten feet. Luke knocked down two jumpers and the nine-point lead had shrunk to five by the end of the quarter. Neither Trent nor I had done much of anything, but O'Leary left us out there.

For the first few minutes of the second quarter, we kept on doing nothing. Roosevelt's lead grew back to eleven. I felt as if I was running in mud—working hard but not getting anywhere. I knew Trent felt the same way; I could see the frustration in his eyes.

It was a fast break off a missed three-pointer that got us untracked. Trent snagged the long rebound, hit me with a quick outlet, and then filled the lane on the left. I took the ball up the center of the court, faked to Luke on the right, then gave a no-look pass to Trent. He caught the ball and in one motion laid the ball off the glass. The lone Roughrider back was totally spun around, but he still managed to foul Trent. I gave Trent a hard high-five, and his eyes were scary. I knew the Roughriders were in for it.

After that fast break he dominated them. It wasn't just his strength either; it was his will. He wanted the rebounds more than anybody else, and he got them. And once he got them, he whistled outlet passes to me and I drove the ball down Roosevelt's throat. I was the point guard, which meant I was supposed to distribute the ball to everybody. Luke got it sometimes, and so did Carver. But whenever there was a choice, I fed the ball to Trent. By the half we'd taken a five-point lead, and by the end of the third quarter we'd stretched it to sixteen.

When the lead hit twenty-two O'Leary took us both out. As we left the court, cheers poured down from the bleachers. Trent returned to the bench and pulled a towel over his head. But I looked up into the stands and pumped my fist into the air.

Chapter 10 At the next practice O'Leary moved Trent and me to the first team, and the up-tempo style that suited us was back, too.

There is nothing I like more than creating in the open

court, and Trent had become a dream finisher. I fed him the ball again and again. Everything was working for him: the drives, the jumper, even the three-pointer.

At the end of practice, O'Leary had me wait on the court until all the guys were in the locker room. "That was solid, Nick. Real solid," he said. "I like the way you and Trent play. You have a feel for each other, and that's something you can't coach."

"We've been practicing together," I explained. "I know where and when he likes the ball."

"Yeah? Well, that's good. That's real good. Only don't forget about Luke and Darren. Those guys can score too, and they get itchy when they're not getting their shots."

"Trent was hot today," I said, defending myself. "So I got him the ball. I'll get them the ball when they're hot."

He nodded. "Fair enough. Find the hot hand and feed it — you do that and you'll be starting at point guard for the next three years. Guaranteed. Now go shower up."

I started off the court, my spirits soaring, when he called out to me again. "Hey, Nick, have they caught Trent's crazy brother?"

"No," I answered. "They haven't."

He frowned. "Well, I hope they do. And soon."

The victory over Roosevelt was just the beginning. Against Woodinville Trent had ten rebounds and twenty-two points, while I added eight points and dished out eight assists. The Juanita Rebels were next. Again Trent had a double double — twenty-four points and eleven rebounds. I handed out nine assists, seven of them to him. After that we avenged our earlier loss to the Eastlake Wolves, then beat the two dogs of our league, Redmond and Lake Washington. Our overall record was a mediocre 8–6, but in the league we were 8–3, and we still had two games left against first-place Garfield.

You put together a winning streak like that, and the locker room should be a wild place. Guys singing, towels snapping, water splashing everywhere. But the energy in our locker room wasn't that much greater than when we'd been losing. Sure, guys congratulated each other, said "Good game" and all that. But they dressed quickly and left in little groups of two and three.

On the day of our first game against Garfield, I was sitting alone eating a grilled cheese sandwich and soup in the cafeteria. Luke spotted me and came over. "You mind if I sit here?"

"No problem," I said, glad for the company.

We talked about the food, the game coming up, school. I wanted to relax, have it be the way it was early in the year, but there was a tightness to his jaw that made me uncomfortable. He had something to say, something I wasn't going to like. He finished off his milk shake and put the cup down on the table. "We can't keep winning this way, you know."

"What do you mean?" I asked, even though I knew.

He tipped the empty cup back and forth. "Come on, Nick. The other coaches aren't stupid. They read the papers, check the box scores, scout the games. It's Trent and you, and the rest of us just run up and down the court. That works against lousy teams, but a great team like Garfield will shut one or both of you down, and that'll be that."

"It hasn't happened yet," I said.

"It will. We're not a real team, Nick."

His words hung there for a moment, like a ball hanging on the rim. I swallowed. "Okay. If you get open, I'll get you the ball. The same thing with Darren, with everybody."

Luke stuck his hand out across the table. I reached out and shook it. Then he left.

I finished my lunch alone. The tomato soup was watery, the milk was warm, and the grilled cheese looked and tasted like yellow rubber. It was the best-tasting lunch I'd had in weeks.

Chapter 11 Garfield. You just say the name around Seattle and people think *basketball*. That's how good they are. We'd originally been scheduled to play them in December, but then they'd been invited to some super-tournament tournament in Washington, D.C. So now we were going to face them twice inside three weeks.

The first game was at their school, which is in the heart of the Central District in Seattle. No Bothell Cougar team had ever won there. As soon as we pulled into the parking lot, I knew why.

Everything about inner-city high schools is different from schools in the suburbs. At Bothell our buildings are all one story. The campus roams around for blocks. There are baseball fields and football fields west of the school, tennis courts on the north, garden spaces and grassy picnic areas in between the buildings. Fancy murals decorate the walls; tile pavers edge the walkways.

All of Garfield High was squeezed into one city block. The main building consisted of three stories of tired-looking brick and wood. The halls had a musty smell; the ceilings and walls had holes where plaster had fallen down and stains where rain had leaked through the roof. The porcelain sinks in the locker room were yellow with age. You wouldn't think stuff like that would matter to a basketball game. A court is a court. But little things can throw you out of your comfort zone, make you nervous and edgy.

When we took the court, it only got worse. Bothell High has about twenty black kids in the whole school; Garfield has more like a thousand. Right behind our bench was our band, and then clustered around them were Bothell parents and students—though not too many had actually come. Almost all of those faces were white. The rest of the gym was a sea of black and brown faces, with a few white faces here and there. I know it shouldn't matter, that people are people and all that. But you can't tell me that the Garfield guys feel at home when they're playing in a gym packed with white people.

I looked around at my teammates and their faces were pasty. Even Luke looked scared. That surprised me—I figured he'd be the one guy who'd be okay. Then I remembered what he told me about his fancy house in Atlanta, and I thought about the big house he had in Bothell. He was as much of a stranger to the inner city as I was.

We started the game scared, which means we started soft. We got up on them on defense, but not all the way up. We went after rebounds, but not with every ounce of energy. It was as if we were pitching pennies for some big prize at the fair. We expected to come close; but we didn't expect to win. We would have been satisfied to keep the score close, lose by eight or ten, just so long as we weren't blown out.

Everybody except Trent. He wasn't intimidated: not by the gym, not by the fans, not by the Garfield players. In the first quarter he single-handedly kept us in the game, scoring six points and pulling down just about every rebound we got. In the last thirty seconds, I knocked down one long three-pointer, and Luke threw up a prayer that banked in as the horn sounded. Those two baskets cut Garfield's lead to six points — we were lucky it wasn't sixteen.

O'Leary rested Trent at the start of the second quarter, and with him out, the six-point lead grew to twelve, then fifteen. The Garfield crowd was going crazy. It felt like an earthquake was ripping through the gym.

O'Leary called time-out to get Trent back in, and to settle the rest of us down. "You can play with these guys," he said as we huddled around him. "All you've got to do is believe in yourselves!"

That was the problem: we didn't. After the time-out, the gym got even louder. On Garfield's next possession my knees were so wobbly that my guy blew by me on a drive to the hoop. It looked like another easy bucket until Trent came flying across the court, blocking the shot but fouling the guy so hard he crumpled to the floor. Instead of reaching down to help him up, Trent turned away. "Cover your guy!" he barked at me. I nodded, then looked to the Garfield player who was just getting to his feet. He was staring wide-eyed at Trent, and so were the other Garfield guys.

Right after that we started chipping at the lead. We didn't go on any big run, but we did play our game. Trent was a force on the glass at both ends of the court, and my passes were crisp and clean. We ran a lot of two-man stuff—inside, outside—and it worked. By the half the Bulldogs' lead was down to nine. If we just kept doing what we were doing, we could win.

I hadn't figured on Garfield changing things.

But they did. First time down the court in the third quarter, I lobbed an entry pass into Trent on the lower blocks. Immediately they hit him with a double-team. Luke broke to the hoop and was wide open for a split second, but Trent lowered his shoulders and tried to spin left and then right. All he managed to do was travel with the ball.

It wasn't a one-time thing, either. On the next four possessions, every time Trent touched the ball Garfield ran a double-team at him, and he either walked or threw the ball away or forced up a bad shot. Garfield's lead soared back into double digits.

It was after Trent's third foul that Luke clapped his hands together and glared at me, his eyes saying, *Get me the ball!* Carver had the same look in his eyes. O'Leary was up shouting at me. "Don't force it, Abbott!"

Garfield's big center missed a sweeping hook, Luke grabbed the rebound and passed to me. There was no fast-break opportunity, but I pushed the ball up quickly. Trent had hustled down and posted up on the right side. He looked open, which was the beauty of Garfield's double-team. He always looked open, but once I made the entry pass they closed on him. I faked the pass in. Luke's guy bit, taking a step toward Trent. Immediately I whipped a bullet pass to Luke. He caught it and in one motion rose for the open fifteen-footer. It was money in the bank, and he gave me a nod as we hustled down to play defense.

Next time it was Carver's turn. Then I went back to Luke, into McShane. Moving the ball, moving it, always moving it, all through the third quarter and into the fourth. Late in the fourth Trent set up down low. I lobbed the ball in, just to see. The double-team didn't come. Trent gave an up-fake, rolled to the hoop, and powered up a short jumper that banked through.

Garfield's coach called time-out. I looked up at the scoreboard. The score was tied at sixty-two with sixteen seconds left. Garfield's fans were up all through the time-out, but they weren't cheering. They were stunned. O'Leary barked directions at us. "Two-three zone defense! You understand! No penetration! Make them shoot outside, and when they do, hit the boards!" The horn sounded and we were back on the court.

O'Leary's switch to a zone was a brilliant stroke. We'd played man-to-man defense the whole way, and the two-three confused the Garfield guards. As the clock wound down, they looked at each other, unsure what play to run. Ten seconds, then eight, then six.

166

The Garfield guard panicked, forcing the ball inside where there was no one open. Carver got a hand on it, controlled it. He hit me with a quick outlet, and I was off, leading a three-on-one break with Trent on my right and Luke on my left.

I drove hard into the lane. I faked to Trent's side, the defender bit, and I dished the ball to Luke, a soft pass right in his hands. He caught it in stride, soared upward in the same fluid motion, and gently laid the ball against the backboard. It dropped through the net just as the horn sounded. A tenth of a second later we were jumping all over him.

For the first time, the celebration carried into the locker room. Guys were howling with joy, drumming on the lockers, laughing and laughing. Even Trent joined in. He didn't scream or anything, but he was smiling, and he didn't shower quickly and dress off by himself as if he were a visitor who'd somehow wandered into the wrong locker room.

"Wasn't that great!" I said to him as we came out of the locker room and headed toward my mother's car.

Before he could answer, a police car pulled into the parking light, its lights flashing. We both froze as two policemen got out and walked across the parking lot right toward us, flashlights piercing the darkness. When they went right past us, I breathed of sigh of relief. "For a second there I thought they were after us," I said, trying to make a joke of it.

On the drive back to Bothell I tried to get Trent talking about his game, but his sentences were short and his eyes kept peering into the dark streets.

Chapter 12 First thing Sunday morning Luke phoned. "Some of the guys are coming over tonight," he said. "My dad's going to make us some burgers, then we're going to watch the North Carolina–Duke game. Interested?"

"Sure," I said. "Sounds great."

"Really?" he said.

I laughed. "Yeah. Really. Unless you don't want me."

"No, I want you to come. I just didn't think you would."

"Well, I will," I said. "What time?"

"Around six-thirty." He paused. "And Nick, see if you can get Trent to come. It'd be great to get the whole team together."

As soon as I hung up, the phone rang again. This time it was Dad. "You doing anything today?"

An hour later we were at Alderwood Mall checking out basketball shoes. What I wanted was the Gary Payton model, but they were expensive. He saw me eyeing them. "Those," he said to the salesman, "in size eleven, medium width." When the salesman walked away, Dad looked to me. "When you're a star, you dress the part."

After he paid we found our way to the food court. I must have thanked him five times for the shoes while we ate our burritos. "You want to do something to pay me back?" he said after the fifth time.

"Yeah, sure," I replied. "What is it?"

He leaned toward me, his voice not much above a whisper. "Look for your own shot more often. If you do, you'll open the court..." He went on and on, giving me his same old lecture. It was as if our roles had somehow been reversed. He

168

was the little kid rattling on, and I was the adult nodding my head and pretending to listen. There was no way I could do what he wanted me to do. No way.

It was three in the afternoon when he dropped me off in front of my house. I went inside and saw Katya and Scott on the sofa, practicing together. It had been a long time since she'd been around our house. "Hey, how's it going?" I asked.

"Okay," she answered, and she didn't seem angry with me.

I sucked up my courage. "How's Michael doing?"

"He's okay. He gets tired easily, but that's normal. The doctors say he'll make a complete recovery."

"That's great." I almost added that I'd stop by and see him, but I caught myself.

Around six I headed over to Trent's. I knocked on his door, but there was no answer. I waited, then knocked again. Finally the door opened. His mother, wearing a bathrobe and smoking a cigarette, stood before me.

"You want Trent?" she asked.

"Yeah," I answered. "If he's around."

"He's around." She turned and hollered his name into the house. Then she looked back to me. "You're Nick, right?"

I nodded.

"Nick from the basketball team? Nick that he shoots around at night with."

Again I nodded.

She took a drag on her cigarette, blew out the smoke. "Tell me, Nick, is Trent any good at basketball?"

"Yeah, he's good," I said. "Really good. And he's getting

better all the time. You should come to a game and see for yourself."

She didn't smile, but she was interested. "And how about this school stuff? How's he doing with that?"

"He's better at math than I am. And he does okay in the other subjects."

She shook her head. "My son, the scholar-athlete. Who'd'a thunk it?" There was sarcasm in her voice, but there was pride too.

Behind her I saw Trent come down the stairs, taking them two at a time. She turned back into the house. In the living room I could see a duffel bag, half-packed, the zippers still open, clothes spilling out. Trent caught me looking at it. He picked it up, slung it to the side of the room, stepped onto the porch, and pulled the door closed behind him. "What's up?"

"Luke is having everybody over for a barbecue. I thought you might want to come."

He shook his head. "Not interested."

"Come on," I persisted, trying to sound casual. "It's a team party. And there's going to be tons of good food. We can't have a team party without our main man."

"I told you. I'm not interested."

A second later I was staring at his front door.

You get a door slammed in your face, and a lot of thoughts come to mind—none of them nice. As I walked to Luke's house, I ran through about fifty things I wanted to say to Trent, and all fifty of them were things I'd never want my mother to hear. Before I knew it I'd reached Luke's. The door popped open. "Hey, Nick. What's up?"

I shrugged.

"No Trent?"

"No Trent."

He grabbed me by the arm and pulled me in. "That's all right. I'm glad you came. Glad you came." He led me to the stairway leading down to his rec room. "Most of the other guys are here already."

I walked down. Carver, McShane, Markey, Fabroa, and the rest were sprawled out on sofas and chairs all through Luke's rec room. They called out to me, smiles on their faces, acting as if we'd all been best friends for years.

Luke's dad was out on the deck, wearing a parka and a ski cap, cooking hamburgers on a huge gas barbecue. I went to the sliding glass door and tapped. He looked up. "Long time no see," he called through the glass.

It had been a long time.

I returned to the main part of the room and claimed the last empty seat on the sofa facing the TV. I pointed to a tray of food in front of Darren Carver. "Pass me some chips and pretzels and one of those Cokes, will you?"

Luke heard. "You probably going to have to grab that stuff yourself," he joked. "Everybody knows Darren can't pass. All he knows how to do is shoot." It was a dumb joke, but the guys howled as if it were the funniest thing they'd ever heard, and I howled along with them.

A few minutes later the door to the deck opened and Luke's dad brought in a platter full of burgers. I loaded up my own plate, then sat down again to watch the game. Guys were stuffing themselves and razzing one another at the same time.

After that I relaxed. I ate three hamburgers and a huge bag of chips while I argued with Fabroa about North Carolina's chances to win the national championship. When the game ended, I shot pool with McShane and Luke, then played poker with Carver and Chang.

The next thing I knew Luke's mom was blinking the lights like an elementary schoolteacher. "I hate to break up the party, but you boys all have school tomorrow. And practice afterwards. And two big games this week."

Everyone groaned. I looked at my watch and saw it was after ten. At the door Luke pulled me aside. "Glad you made it, Nick."

Part
Five

Chapter 1

A point guard has to go with the flow of the game. If that means passing the ball five times in a row to the same player, then that's what it means. But he's got to recognize changes in the flow, too, because no game stays the same. It's as if a team is a river spilling down out of the mountains, all the water searching for the easiest path.

That's what I did in the next three games, and we clicked. Luke and Carver ran the court, had good range with the jump shot, and played solid defense. In the low post McShane wasn't a scoring threat, but he didn't have to be. All he had to do was take up space, rebound, and put some hard fouls on anybody trying to drive the key.

Then there was Trent. You'd think with the passes I was making to other guys, his game would suffer. But once I started spreading the ball around, he got his opportunities at the best times — when he was able to operate. If a team put a quick guard on him, Trent would post him up and shoot over him. If a team used a power forward, he'd step back and nail jumper after jumper. No matter who guarded him, he did the dirty work—diving for the loose balls, setting the solid picks, sweeping the glass clean. Those games—against Inglemoor, Edmonds, Roosevelt—went by in a blur. We didn't just win; we dominated.

I should have been on top of the world, but every time I looked at Trent, I got an empty feeling in my gut. Zack hadn't disappeared. He was out there, somewhere. He'd call, sometime. With Trent there was no telling how far we could go. Without him the winning streak and our shot at the league title were gone: buzzer sounds, game over, lights out. The call was coming; I just prayed to God that his phone wouldn't ring until the season had ended.

Chapter 2 We had two games left—one against

Franklin and then the rematch with Garfield. Win them both and we were league champions, the first title for Bothell High in twenty-seven years.

And it was right then, right when everybody most needed to pull together, that Trent started falling apart. On Monday, before practice, he was snarling at everybody in the locker room. Then, going for a rebound during the shoot-around— the shoot-around!—he went over the back of Brian Chang, sending Chang down hard. "What was that all about?" Chang demanded, pulling himself off the ground.

For an answer Trent faked a hard chest pass in Chang's direction. Chang flinched, and Trent laughed in his face.

The attitude continued into the scrimmage. Trent didn't hustle after loose balls; he dogged the fast breaks. He was so out of it that twice in a row Markey took baseline on him, both times driving all the way to the hoop for uncontested lay-ins. When it happened a third time, Matt turned on Trent. "In your face!" he shouted, pumping his fist.

Trent went ballistic. He drove into Markey the way a blitzing linebacker drives into a quarterback, knocking him down and then pummeling him with fists to the stomach. O'Leary, his face bright red, started blowing his whistle; guys jumped in to yank them apart. The whole thing couldn't have taken more than thirty seconds, but it seemed like forever before McShane, Luke, and I pulled him off.

"Take a shower, Dawson," O'Leary shouted, when Trent was finally off Markey.

Trent glared at O'Leary.

"I said take a shower!"

He stomped off the court.

Markey was leaning over, holding his stomach. "What's with him? Is he crazy?"

After dinner that night, Scott and I cleared the table and washed the dishes. Then Scott went to his room. I didn't have much homework—ten problems in math, four questions in history. I brought my books to the kitchen table just as I always did.

I knew Trent wasn't coming. I knew it in my bones. But every time I heard anything, and sometimes when I didn't, I'd look to the back door, hoping to hear his knock.

When I finished the last history question, I pulled on a sweatshirt, grabbed my basketball, and headed out to the back yard to shoot around.

It was cold and growing colder, my shots weren't dropping, and I suddenly felt disgusted with everything. What was I doing out there by myself, shooting hoops in the dark?

I grabbed the ball and started back into the house. But that wasn't right either. I put the ball down on the back porch, went through the gate, crossed the street, and pounded on Trent's front door.

There was a light on in the back, and my pounding caused two more to go on. Finally the door opened a crack. I could barely see him. "We've got to talk," I said.

"About what?"

"Come off it, Trent. You act crazy at practice, you don't show up to shoot hoops. What's happening?"

His mouth turned downward. I could feel him deciding. Finally he pushed the screen door open. "All right," he said, "come in. But you've got to be real quiet. My mother is sleeping upstairs."

It was the first time I'd been inside his house since we'd played pool on his little toy table more than a year before. It didn't look like the house had been cleaned since then. Mail-order catalogs were still strewn around the living room floor. Cigarette butts still spilled out of a paper cup and onto the coffee table. Plates with dried food on them sat on top of the television set. He caught me looking around. "Nice place, isn't it?"

I sat on the sofa and he dropped into a chair across from me. "Did he call?" I asked.

He nodded toward the duffel bag I'd seen before. "Yeah, he called."

My throat went so dry that it was hard for me to swallow. "You think it's smart to go?" I asked. "I mean, aren't the police still watching you? Won't you lead them right to him?"

He laughed. "The police aren't watching me, Nick. Why should they be? Ushakov got shot with a little tiny bullet from a little tiny gun. It wasn't much worse that getting hit with a BB. No big deal. "

"No big deal?" My voice rose with each word. "Who do you think you're kidding? Two or three inches and Michael would be dead."

"Keep it down!" he snapped, looking toward the stairway. "I told you my mother is sleeping."

I took a deep breath. When I spoke again it was in a whisper. "I don't get it. I know you love basketball, love playing. And you're good at it, really good. So why throw it away for Zack? What's he ever done for you?"

He looked down. "Plenty."

"Like what?" I said.

"You really want to know?"

"Yeah," I said. "I really want to know."

He leaned forward, his elbows on his knees. It seemed forever before he spoke, but it probably was only ten seconds. "What's your earliest memory, Nick?"

"I don't know for sure," I answered, thrown off by the

question. "I guess my dad swinging me at the park. Why?"

"Your dad swinging you at the park." He laughed softly. "Well, here's mine. I was three years old, and it was morning, and I was hungry. I went into my mom's room and found her lying naked on the bed next to some guy I'd never seen before. I shook her a couple of times, but she was so drunk or stoned I couldn't wake her up. So I woke up Zack. And what was he? Five years old? Six? The first thing he did was to close the door to my mom's bedroom. Then he led me to the kitchen, got up on a chair, and brought down a big bag of pretzels. Next he went to the refrigerator, and he got out two cans of Coke. He poured the Coke into glasses and spilled those pretzels onto paper plates. And we sat there and had breakfast together." He paused. "All my life he's gotten me the bag of pretzels. Now he's out there alone. You think I can leave him like that?"

We both sat there in the near dark for a long time. "Look," I said at last. "Stay two more games. That's all. At least see the season to the end. Then, if you want, go. Though I still don't see how screwing up your own life is going to help him any."

"You really want to win, don't you?"

That made me mad. "Oh, come off it, Trent. We've come this far. I want to play it out to the end, and you do too. I know you. One week more. That's all I'm asking. One week."

"All right, Nick. One week. But then I'm gone."

Chapter 3 "You've got bags under your eyes," Mom said to me the next morning at breakfast.

"I had a tough night," I admitted.

She frowned. "I'll be glad when basketball season is over. It's absolutely wearing you out."

"This is going to surprise you," I said, "but I will be too."

I didn't see Trent as I walked to school. And I didn't see him before the bell either. My head started pounding. What if he'd been blowing smoke in my face to get me off his back and then had taken off as soon as I'd left? What then?

Then, just before first-period class was about to start, he walked in, sat down in his usual seat, and nodded as if it were any other day.

Instead of feeling better, I felt worse—dizzy somehow—as if I were on a ship in a storm. The ground didn't feel solid under my feet. In history I forgot the years of the Civil War; in English I was on the wrong story. When it came time to pay at lunch, I stood there looking at the woman until the kid behind me nudged me. "You waiting for somebody to buy it for you?"

After school I couldn't get my hall locker open until the fourth try. By the time I was on the court for practice, O'Leary already had Trent in the coaches' office. As the rest of us shot lay-ins, we could see him giving Trent a good chewing-out. When the two of them finally emerged, O'Leary called us all to him. "Trent has something to say," he announced.

Trent looked right at Matt Markey. "Sorry about yesterday," he said, sticking out his hand. "It won't happen again."

Markey shook his hand. "Forget it."

"All right then," O'Leary growled. "Let's get back to basketball."

That was exactly what I wanted to do.

We had a monster practice. The second string played tougher than the teams we'd been crushing. Our passes were crisp, and our shots found the bottom of the net. In the locker room afterwards the guys were sky high. "Two more," McShane shouted. "Two more."

Others took up the chant. *"Two more! Two more! Two more!"* They were still chanting when Trent closed up his locker and slipped out the door.

Chapter 4 And then it was Thursday: Game day. The halls of Bothell High buzzed with excitement. Kids I didn't even know were coming up to me. "Go get 'em!"..."You can do it!"..."We're behind you!"

Game time was seven-thirty. I was in the locker room dressing at six-thirty when Trent came in. He nodded to me, but that was it.

The other guys filed in one-by-one. They were nervous, not talking much. In our first game against Franklin, Trent and I had scored all those points when they weren't taking us seriously. There'd be no sneaking up on them tonight. Half an hour before game time O'Leary went to the blackboard. The chalk banged as he spelled out, in huge capitals, the word TEAM. Then he put about ten exclamation points next to it, smacking the blackboard so hard that the chalk finally broke in half, one piece flying across the room. "This is it, gentlemen. This is what we've been working for. This game. These couple of hours. All of us, together."

Everything moved quickly then. The door leading to the court was thrown open and I was swept along into the throbbing gym. We did our passing drill; the ball boys threw out a half dozen balls and we shot around. The horn sounded, and the next thing I knew the second-stringers were moving to the bench and, along with Darren and Tom, Luke and Trent, I headed to center court. Then the toss went up and the ball came to me. The instant I touched it, I came alive from head to toe. The whole world was a rectangle ninety feet long and fifty feet wide, and what happened inside it made sense.

It's tough to run the fast break early in a big game. The defense is pumped. At every practice, all they've heard is "Get back on defense." Nobody is tired, nobody is discouraged, everybody is hustling. You can blow a team out of a game late in the half or early in the third quarter. But in the first quarter, it's your set offense that's got to carry you.

I'd always run our set offense through Trent, and I started out that night doing the same. But Franklin had scouted us; the second Trent touched the ball, they ran a swarming double-team trap at him.

He didn't panic and he didn't force stuff. He did exactly what he was supposed to do, which was zip the ball back to me. I swung it around to the open man—usually Luke or Darren—on the weak side. Time after time they had good looks at the hoop. Fifteen, eighteen footers, the kind of shots they could make in their sleep. Only now they couldn't get anything to drop.

After three minutes we were down six points. O'Leary called time-out. "Relax," he said to Luke and Darren. "You can make those shots."

But they didn't.

That made Franklin's double-team all the more tenacious. Two Franklin guys would totally commit to Trent every time he touched the ball. They'd even double-team him on rebounds to keep him off the glass. He couldn't score, he couldn't rebound, and Luke and Darren kept missing four out of every five shots they took. Our fans had filled the gym; they were dying to scream their lungs out. But there was nothing to cheer. Franklin's lead grew to seven by the end of the first quarter, eleven at the end of the second.

The locker room at the half was a morgue. Twice O'Leary went to the blackboard and started to write something. Both times he stopped. Finally he smacked the blackboard with his piece of chalk. The noise snapped us to attention. "Gentlemen," he said, his eyes scanning the room, "I know you're hustling, giving me one hundred percent. I'm not faulting anybody's effort. If anything, you're trying too hard. Be yourselves. Play your game."

But the third quarter wasn't all that different from the first half. Franklin stuck with their game plan—double-teaming Trent. I stuck with ours—working the ball to the open guy. But Darren and Luke stayed cold. Their shooting percentage must have been below twenty. Franklin's eleven-point lead grew to fourteen. The score was 53–39 when the horn sounded ending the third quarter.

We had to try something different, and I knew what it was. On our first possession of the fourth quarter, I dumped the ball into Trent; the double-team came; he popped the ball back out. Darren was open to my right, but instead of dishing it to him, I stepped back behind the arc and fired off a three-pointer. I had a nice stroke on the ball, good backspin, good height. It was like all those shots in my back yard—absolutely in the heart.

Franklin missed their shot, and again I brought the ball down. This time I didn't even dump it in. I went to the top of the key, set my feet, and let it fly. Perfect—another three-pointer, the net again snapping as the ball swished through. Our fans came out of their seats with a roar. We'd played twenty seconds and Franklin's fourteen-point lead was down to eight.

The Franklin point guard brought the ball up. I'd been matched up against him all game, and all game he'd been totally in control, cocky even. But now there was something different about him. I could see a little doubt in his eyes, a little fear. Two three-pointers in your face will do that to you. He was tentative with his entry pass. I got a hand on it, deflecting it forward. Darren picked it up and raced toward the hoop. I trailed behind. He drove to the hoop, went up, and then left a soft little pass for me. I was so surprised I actually fumbled it a little. But I got it under control and cozied in the lay-in. Eight straight points—Franklin by six.

They scored on their next trip, slowing our run. But they

didn't regain the momentum. I made sure of that with two more hoops in the next couple of minutes. The game that looked out of reach was back within our grasp—and with plenty of time left.

Their coach called time-out. "Look for a change in their defense," O'Leary warned us. "They're going to come after you, Nick. I'm sure of it. So don't force things. If you're not open, pass the ball."

O'Leary called it exactly right. For the rest of the game Franklin smothered me. But confidence is as contagious as fear. Luke nailed a jumper from the corner. Trent scored on a running eight-footer. Darren sank a set shot from beyond the arc, and our crowd went crazy because for the first time in the game we had the lead. Then came another jumper from the corner by Darren. A miss by Trent, but a put-back by McShane. The baskets poured down like rain.

Just before the buzzer I sunk a final three-pointer, pushing the final margin to twelve. The horn sounded and we raced off the court, arms raised above our heads, as our fans chanted: "We're number one! We're number one!"

Chapter 5 In the locker room all the guys surrounded me. "Great game, Nick! Way to step up!" I expected that from Luke and Trent, but to hear it from Carver and McShane, from Fabroa and Markey and Chang—that was the greatest feeling. I tried to act as if what I'd done was no big deal, but I thought I was going to bust apart. I sat soaking up their praise for so long that when everybody else was long gone, I was still in my underwear.

I finished dressing and left the locker room. Dad was waiting for me, a big grin on his face. He wanted to go out for pizza, but suddenly I felt really, really tired. "If it's okay, Dad," I said, "I just want to go home."

"Come on, Nick! This is what we've been waiting for, isn't it? Let's go out, celebrate, talk. You and me."

"I'm tired."

He stiffened. "All right. You call the shots."

It's a five-minute ride from the high school to our house. He looked over at me a couple of times. "Something wrong?" he asked as we neared the house.

"Nothing's wrong."

I knew Scott would be with Katya, but I thought Mom would be home. She wasn't though, which was fine with me. I wanted to be by myself.

I went to the kitchen and got some chocolate chip cookies and a glass of milk. I sat at the kitchen table, enjoying the quiet, the cookies, the cold milk.

My mind wandered, jumping here and there. I remembered the shots, the passes, Franklin's early lead. Then I was in the locker room, before the game, looking at the blackboard and the one word O'Leary had written. TEAM. I'd heard it a million times, but I'd never really understood what it meant before. Seniors and sophomores, first-stringers and bench warmers, we were all one, all doing things together that we couldn't have done on our own. It was a great feeling, a feeling I didn't want to give up.

That's when I knew I had to go see Trent one last time.

It was crazy in a way. Three months earlier I'd have been glad to have him leave—in fact, I would have bought him his ticket. But now I knew him. His crooked smile, the way he took stairs two at a time, his stutter-step dribble on drives to the hoop. I knew him. And when you know somebody, everything changes. I looked out the window. There was a light on downstairs. I laced up my shoes, headed across the street, and tapped on his door. Immediately it opened up; he peered out through the screen.

"You got a minute?" I asked.

He stepped out onto the porch. "I guess. What's up?"

I thought for a moment, wanting to pick my words carefully. "I just want to know how things stand," I said.

He looked at me, his face blank. "I'm still going, if that's what you're asking."

"But why?" I said. "You don't want to go. I know you don't."

He looked away. "It's not a question of what I want to do."

I thought for a while, trying to get the words just right. "So he looked out for you when you were little. Okay? Nobody's arguing. He was a good brother. But that was a long time ago, Trent. You can't mess up your own life because Zack gave you pretzels and a can of Coke twelve years ago. It doesn't make any sense."

His eyes flashed. "I already told you I'd stay for the Garfield game."

"I'm not talking about the Garfield game. I'm talking about everything. The hoops at night in the back yard, the school

188

stuff. Everything. The summer, and next season, and the season after that."

He shook his head. "You don't get it, do you?"

"No, I don't," I said, my voice rising. "I don't get it."

He shook his head. "I just don't fit with guys like you. I never have and I never will."

"You don't fit with Zack," I said. "Not anymore."

He looked away. "You don't know everything, Nick. If you did, you wouldn't say that."

Something in his voice scared me, but I'd gone too far to back off. "So tell me. Make me understand."

For a long time he didn't speak. Finally he nodded. "All right, I'll tell you. I'll tell you everything." He paused, and his voice dropped to a whisper. "Zack wasn't alone when he killed those birds. I was right there with him. I killed half of them, maybe more. I hit them with a golf club, hit them over and over until they were dead. I don't know why I did it. I just did it. But Zack never told the cops I was there. He took all the heat. You hear me? All of it. And the shooting? That was my fault. Because once Zack got out I rode him, telling him he had to do something to get back at Ushakov, something big. I watched him get the gun down from the closet, saw him flip through the yellow pages looking for a place to buy bullets. I knew where he was going that night, what he was planning. I could have stopped him. All it would have taken was one word from me. But I let him go. I wanted to roll the dice, see what would happen."

He stopped then, stopped and stared at me. I knew I should have said something, but a numbness had come over me. I felt light-headed, dizzy. He went on. "Now you tell me, Nick. Do you think your mom would have me in her house if she knew? Do you think Luke's dad would have me over for a barbecue?"

"You've changed, Trent," I said, finally finding my voice. "You're different from what you used to be."

He snorted in disgust. "Nothing changes, Nick. Nothing and nobody."

I swallowed. "So the team, you and me being friends, all we've gone through—it doesn't count for anything?"

He shook his head slowly. "It doesn't count for anything."

I stared at him for a while. "If that's how you feel," I said at last, "then don't wait until after the Garfield game. Go as soon as you can. Tonight even." With that I turned and headed across the street toward my own house.

Chapter 6 I hardly slept that night. Sometimes I told myself that I had done the right thing, the only thing. A minute later I'd be certain I'd totally blown it. It was probably three A.M. before I fell asleep, which made the alarm at six that much crueler.

When I stepped outside the door to head to school, I peered over at Trent's house. It looked empty, but it often looked empty. I almost went over and knocked on his front door, just to see if he was still there, but then I decided to let it go.

Before my first-period class Martha Judkins came over and told me what a good game I'd played, how exciting it was to watch, how she'd never been much of a basketball fan before. Any other day I'd have been ecstatic to have her standing by my desk, leaning her body close. But that day I kept looking past her to the door, which kept opening and closing, hoping the next person would be Trent.

The bell rang. That's when I started lying to myself. Big deal that he wasn't there. If I'd had any sense, I'd have stayed home, too. He was probably sound asleep. The talk about taking off to go live with Zack—it was all talk. He had a room and a bed and a mother who left him alone. Why would he go live on the streets?

At lunch Luke and Darren came right over to me. "Where's Trent?" Luke asked. "Nobody's seen him all day."

I shrugged. "I guess he cut school."

"Today?" Darren said in disbelief.

"He'll be at practice, won't he?" Luke said. "He wouldn't cut that."

"Sure," I answered. "He'll be at practice."

But he wasn't. As the guys suited up, I could see them looking around, wondering. On the court, a rack of basketballs was waiting for us. Pretty soon guys were dribbling and shooting, doing the normal loosening up that we'd been doing for three months. To an outsider things would have looked totally normal. But each time one of the gym doors opened, everybody stopped to look, hoping to see Trent.

Coach O'Leary emerged from his office, blew his whistle. We circled around him. He scanned our faces. "Where's Dawson?" No one answered. He looked at me. "Was he in school today?"

I shook my head. "No, Coach."

His forehead wrinkled. "What is he, sick or something?"

"I guess so," I answered.

Practice was light. We walked through our plays, then just shot around. What we needed was rest and O'Leary knew it. When practice ended I headed off the court, but before I reached the locker room O'Leary called me over. "What's up with Dawson?"

I looked down. There was too much to explain, way too much. "Who knows? He's always been tough to figure."

O'Leary frowned. "Check on his house for me, will you? And if he's there, you have him call me. Okay?"

"Okay."

He turned and headed toward his office.

"Coach," I called after him, "what if he's not there?"

He turned back. "Then *you* call me."

Chapter 7 He wasn't. And if his mother was home, she didn't answer. I knocked and called out, then knocked again. Back at my own house I telephoned O'Leary and gave him the news. "Great," he said. "Perfect timing."

At dinner Scott pulled some bread apart, stuck a piece in his mouth, then looked at me. "What's the deal with Dawson?"

When I didn't answer, my mother took up the question. "Is something wrong?"

I shrugged. "I don't know what you're talking about..."

"Come on, Nick. I go to Bothell High too, you know."

"What's going on?" my mother asked.

Scott turned to her. "Trent wasn't at school today. And from the way Nick was pounding on his front door and calling his name out, I'd say that he wasn't at practice either. Which means he probably took off, just like I always said he would."

"And you're happy about it, too, aren't you? You want him to screw up. You can't stand it that things might turn out okay for him."

Scott looked at me hard. "Tell me this, Nick. Would you be so worried if he disappeared after the season was over?"

Any other time I probably would have exploded. But at that moment I was too tired. I dropped my silverware onto the table, pushed my chair back, and stood.

"Where are you going?" Mom asked.

"I'm going to my room. I'm not hungry."

And that's what I did. I went straight to my room and lay on my bed. From downstairs I could hear—or at least I thought I could hear—Mom chewing out Scott.

Then there was silence for a while. A little later I heard the front door open and close—Scott leaving, undoubtedly to go to Katya's. A few minutes after that Mom knocked on my door. "You want to talk?" she asked, her voice soft.

"Not really."

"Well, I do." She came into the room and sat at the end of my bed. "This has been a hard year for Scott, you know."

I laughed. "Yeah? Well, it hasn't exactly been a piece of cake for me either."

"I know, I know. Still, put yourself in his shoes. His younger brother becomes the big star on the team he quit. That's tough."

"So what am I supposed to do about it? Just let him insult me?"

"No, no." She looked out my window for a while, then looked back. "I always want you to remember he's your brother. That's all."

There was a sadness in her voice that took the anger out of me. "I know he's my brother," I said. "It's just that he can be such a . . . oh, I don't know. But I don't hate him, if that's what you're worried about."

Her face relaxed a little; she even smiled. Then she sneaked a peak at her watch. It was Friday night, her night to meet at Starbucks with other women who were going through divorces. "You should go," I said.

"I could skip it. We could rent a movie, pop some popcorn. We haven't done that in a long time."

I shook my head. "I couldn't watch a movie. You go."

She patted me on the leg, then stood. "I love you."

Half an hour later the house was empty. I grabbed my basketball and went outside, not because I wanted to play, but because there was nothing else to do. I don't think I knew I was burning up until I felt the coolness of the night air on my face. I took the ball out to the top of the key, eyed the hoop in the dim light, and let it fly. The sound of the ball ripping through the cords was soothing.

I'd been shooting for about an hour when I thought I heard something from behind our shed. I held the ball and peered into the darkness. We have raccoons sometimes, and cats all the time. But this had sounded different, or maybe I'd just hoped it had. "Trent, are you out there?"

The wind moved the high branches of the hemlock trees. A car drove down 104th. The sounds of a laugh track from a television comedy drifted by. But that was all.

Chapter 8 The Garfield game started at one. At nine in the morning I went over and knocked on Trent's door. I knew it was useless. There was no car in the driveway. The shades were all pulled down.

I was barely back inside my own house when Luke phoned. "Any sign of Trent?"

"No."

A long pause. "Well, I guess we're just going to have to win without him, aren't we?"

"I guess we are."

After I hung up, Mom came out from the kitchen. "Anything?"

I shook my head.

She pursed her lips, then forced herself to smile. "How do pancakes sound? I mixed up some batter."

Normally it's my favorite breakfast, but that morning the idea of doughy pancakes covered with thick syrup turned my stomach. "I'm not up for pancakes," I said. "I'd rather just have some toast if that's okay."

Another smile. "Of course it's okay. I'll put the batter in

the refrigerator. It won't go bad. But is toast going to be enough?"

"It'll have to be. I don't think I could eat much more."

Mom made toast for me, poured me a glass of orange juice, then sat and drank coffee as I ate.

"Where's Scott?" I asked, as I put jam on the toast.

She frowned. "Where do you think?"

When I finished eating I started to wash up, but she stopped me. "I'll do the dishes this morning. It's not every day my son plays for the championship."

While she did the dishes, I sprawled out on the sofa. My head was throbbing and I felt chilled the way you feel when you're about to come down with the flu, so I closed my eyes for a second, opened them, then closed them again.

It was the telephone that woke me. It rang three times before my mother picked it up, or at least three times that I heard.

I could tell from the cool tone of her voice who she was talking to. I stretched my arms above my head and yawned. "Is that Dad?"

"Yes," she said. "Here, he wants to talk to you." She put the telephone down on the table and went into the kitchen, closing the door behind her.

I picked up the phone. "Hello, Dad."

Those were the last words I said for a while. His words spilled out a mile a minute. He told me all sorts of stuff I already knew. My picture had been in the *Seattle Times*; there'd been an article about the team in *Eastside Journal*. Then he told me stuff I didn't know. At work he'd made a bunch of bets with other men who said there was no way that Bothell could beat Garfield twice in one season. "But we know better than that, don't we?"

"Sure," I said.

"And Nick—" There was a long pause then, as if there was something he wanted to say but couldn't put into words.

"Yeah, Dad?" I said.

"Nothing, nothing." Suddenly his tone changed back. "Just go get 'em! You hear me!"

When I hung up, it was after eleven. We were supposed to be in the locker room and dressed by eleven forty-five. I had time, but no extra. I hustled upstairs and packed my gym bag. When I came back downstairs Mom gave me a hug and a kiss on the forehead. "Good luck!" Then she squeezed my arm. "I'm proud of you."

Outside it was mostly gray, but with a little blue in the sky. At the end of my walkway I stopped and looked at Trent's house. The garbage can was lying on its side by the back fence, stray pieces of paper littered the flower beds. It looked just the way it always looked.

Chapter 9 When I opened the door to the locker room, Luke was in his uniform and Darren was lacing up his shoes. No sooner had I sat down in front of my own locker than Coach O'Leary came over. He didn't say anything; the look in his eyes asked the question for him. I shook my head. He turned and went back into the coaches' office.

The locker room quickly filled up. Markey, McShane,

Chang, Fabroa. Each guy came in, looked around for Trent, then dressed.

A few minutes before we took the court, O'Leary went to the chalkboard and laid out the game plan as if nothing were different.

As soon as O'Leary finished, we ran out into the packed gymnasium. The band played the school fight song; cheerleaders yelled into their megaphones; the dance team did flips along the sideline. Two thousand people roared for us.

O'Leary had the team manager bring out the rack of balls. We went through the lay-in line seven or eight times, and then we just shot around.

That's when the questions started. Kids would walk by and call out to us. *"Where's Dawson?"...*"Dawson never showed?"* ...*"Is Dawson hurt?"*

It wasn't just at courtside either. You could hear Trent's name murmured up in the bleachers, in the aisles, all through the gymnasium. I saw a reporter from the *Eastside Journal* talking with O'Leary. Even the Garfield coach kept looking at us, then looking toward the locker room.

The horn sounded—game time. We put our hands together and hollered just as we always did, maybe even louder than usual. At center court we stared down the Garfield guys, trying to be tough.

It didn't take Garfield long to find our weakness. With Trent missing they pounded the ball inside. Their center had twenty pounds on McShane, and he used that weight to muscle McShane out of the way. Their forwards somehow seemed bigger, too. On missed shots they crashed the boards, swinging their elbows, clearing space.

They scored the first five points of the game and at the quarter led by nine. Luke sank a three-pointer on our first possession in the second quarter, and our crowd came alive, but it was then that the Garfield coach hit us with a wave of substitutes.

Their fresh legs turned the game into a rout. My arms were so tired I could hardly lift them over my head. My legs went rubbery; I lost my foot speed, and jump shots that normally found the bottom of the net barely reached the rim. And the other guys were in the same shape.

Garfield went for the kill—running every chance they had, gambling on defense, hounding us full court. And we broke. Not just physically, but mentally. On the final possession of the half, Garfield hauled down four straight offensive rebounds before their center, tired of seeing shots bounce off the rim, powered down a vicious dunk that rocked the backboard just as the horn sounded. We were playing at home, but there was a smattering of boos as we left the court, our shoulders slumped and our heads down. One guy leaned over the railing and hissed: "You suck!"

Inside the locker room guys collapsed onto benches, eyes on the ground. About five times O'Leary looked as if he was going to say something, but every time he was about to start, he stopped.

When I was certain no pep talk was coming, I went to the sink, stuck my head under the faucet, and turned on the cold water. I pulled my head out, gave it a shake, then closed my eyes and toweled myself dry. When my eyes were closed, when the whole world had gone black, I thought of Trent.

I pictured him on a bus somewhere, looking out the window and watching the telephone poles click by. He'd know the game was going on. He'd even be able to tell what quarter we were in by the time. Was he playing the game in his mind? Or did he even care?

O'Leary clapped his hands. "Let's go, gentlemen."

There weren't many cheers when we took the court. The gym was still full, but the tension had gone out of the crowd. Even the band sounded sluggish. The guys were down too, tossing up jumpers as if it were gym class. I thought about calling my teammates together, saying something to them, but you don't lead by talking.

The horn sounded, and I was standing at center court for the tip. I was the point guard. Win or lose, I had to lead.

The ref tossed the ball up; McShane got a piece of it, and then a Garfield guy swatted it toward the scorer's table. The ball was headed out of bounds, but instead of letting it go and hoping for the call, I hustled after it, caught it, spun, and threw it to Markey just as I crashed into the timekeeper. I didn't see how Markey scored; I was picking myself up off the ground when the ball went through the net. But I did hear the roar from the crowd. Markey high-fived me as he hustled back to play defense, and his eyes were alive.

For the first minutes of the third quarter I was all over the place, sometimes saving the ball, more often not. But even when you don't make the great play, hustle pays off. One guy throws his body on the floor and all of a sudden everybody does. Rebounds, loose balls, even the ref's calls, all came our way. Garfield's eighteen-point lead shrank to thirteen, then ten.

Finally their coach called time-out. Our fans gave us a standing ovation. Luke waved a towel in the air, and the crowd roared louder. It was the Garfield guys who were shaking their heads, looking for all the world like a team that was behind, not ahead.

After the time-out our crowd stayed on their feet, yelling, screaming, and stomping on the bleachers. Garfield, clearly rattled, forced a shot. Luke rebounded and hit me with a quick outlet. But they had two guys back, so there was no chance for a fast break.

I walked the ball up the court, all the time looking to Luke's side. The guy guarding me saw my eyes and was lulled by my pace. He was sure I was going to feed Luke. Instead, I put on a burst, blowing right by him. One of their big guys came up to stop me as I reached the key. I crossed over on the dribble and went up for the shot. That's when I got hit. I'm not sure what it was, whether it was an elbow or a shoulder or a forearm. All I know is that my nose was totally flattened, that the blood came gushing, and that there was no whistle.

As I crumpled to the ground, Garfield's center cleared my missed shot. For a second I saw all these feet going by me. I tried to get up, but my mouth was full of blood.

Garfield scored, and immediately the ref blew his whistle,

stopping play. O'Leary came out, gave me a towel to hold to my nose, and helped me to the sideline. I slumped onto the chair and dabbed at my nose to try to get the bleeding to stop. O'Leary knelt in front of me. "You okay?"

"I'm fine...I'm fine," I answered, anxious to get back on the court. But the bleeding wouldn't stop. I looked up to see Garfield score again, this time when my guy drained a three-pointer over Chang. "You've got to put me back in."

O'Leary shook his head. "You know the AIDS rule. The refs can't let you play. Listen, Nick, there's a doctor here. You go back into the locker room with him. He'll get you fixed up."

As I walked down the aisleway toward the locker room, the crowd groaned. Garfield had scored again.

The doctor sat me down on the bench and started squeezing my nose. I winced in pain. "Do you have to do that?"

He kept squeezing. "If you want to play I do." He took some gauze out of a first-aid kit and stuck it up my nose. "There's nothing broken. Lean forward and pinch. I'll be back in a minute."

After he left I sat dabbing at my nose, rotating the towel to get a clean white spot so I'd be able to tell when the bleeding had stopped. I pinched, and pinched harder, but still the tiny drops of blood came.

Time crawled. Finally the locker room door swung open again. I looked up, expecting to see the doctor. I was going to tell him that he had to do something, and fast, but it wasn't him. Standing in front of me, wearing baggy pants and a T-shirt, with his hair slicked back and his duffel bag slung over his shoulder, was Trent. For a split second my body went electric, as if I'd sunk a shot from half court at the buzzer. Then, as quickly as it came, the feeling went.

"What are you doing here?" I asked.

He shrugged. "I don't know exactly. I guess I had to see the game, see how it all ended."

I wasn't sure I understood. "You mean you've been here the whole time?"

He nodded. "Almost. I snuck into the coaches' office right after the game started. It's got that little square window. You can see most of the court, and the scoreboard, and nobody can see you."

"And you just watched?"

"Yeah. I just watched."

I dabbed my nose—no blood. I threw the towel to the ground and stood. "Look, I don't understand why you're here, or what you want from me. But right now I don't have time to find out." With that I pushed by him, hustled up the aisle, and back to the bench.

As I took the chair next to O'Leary, I looked up at the scoreboard. We were down by seventeen with fifty-seven seconds left in the third. Bad, but not as bad as I thought it was going to be.

"You okay?" O'Leary asked, his eyes glued to the action on the court.

"Yeah," I said. "Listen, Coach, there's something I should tell you."

The whistle blew. A foul was called on Garfield's center. O'Leary grabbed my shoulder. "Later. Get in there for Chang." He felt me hesitate. "Go!"

I checked in at the scorer's table, then stepped onto the court. As I did, the people in the bleachers stood and cheered. Puzzled, I looked around trying to figure out what was happening. Luke and Darren were both smiling a little, and I realized that the fans were cheering for me, that they were standing and cheering for me. The hair on the back of my neck rose. I didn't know what to do, so I kind of waved in appreciation. The roar grew louder.

The ref handed the basketball to the Garfield point guard. He in-bounded it and I back-pedaled on defense, looking for a chance to make a steal. I anticipated his pass, broke on the ball, only he didn't throw it. My man went back door for an easy lay in. *Big star,* I thought to myself as I brought the ball upcourt. *Keep that up and they'll stand and boo.*

We held for the last shot, a jumper from the corner by Carver, which rimmed out. With one quarter left in the season, we were down nineteen.

Then, during the quarter break a low murmur went through the gym, a different kind of murmur than I'd heard before. O'Leary stopped midsentence and looked around. So did the other guys. Even the Garfield players stopped, puzzled.

Then the chant began. *"Dawson! Dawson! Dawson!"* We couldn't see him, but our fans could. He was coming up the aisle toward the court. I looked to where I knew he would appear. The seconds ticked away. And then he was there.

He walked toward us, joined the huddle. "Where the hell

have you been?" O'Leary snapped. Before Trent could answer the horn sounded. O'Leary scowled. "Get out there," he snapped. "See if you can do something."

As we took the court I watched the other guys, watched the way they looked at Trent. They weren't mad at Trent, not the way I had been. Confused, bewildered—that's how they looked.

Then Trent, maybe for the first time in his life, did exactly the right thing. He went from player to player, holding up his fist. When each held up his fist in return, Trent lightly tapped his knuckles against theirs. Finally he came to me. His eyes were hard and tough; they would always be hard and tough— the eyes of an outsider. But he was going to play the game, and that's what mattered. We tapped knuckles just as the ref blew his whistle.

On their first possession, Garfield's guard made a terrible pass that went four rows into the stands. The fans went crazy, as if we'd scored twenty unanswered points. I inbounded to Trent and the chant started again. *"Dawson! Dawson! Dawson!"*

Trent took that in-bound pass, dribbled across the time-line, then returned the ball to me and set up in the low blocks. Everybody in the gym knew where the ball was going, including all five Garfield guys. The smart play would have been to fake a pass to him, and hit Luke or Carver. But there are times when things are just fated.

I dumped the ball into Trent. Before the double-team reached him, he gave a quick up-fake and then spun baseline to the bucket. Their center rotated over, but Trent went up anyway and banked home a twelve-footer. I thought the roof would come off the gym, that's how loud the cheer was. *"Dawson! Dawson! Dawson!"*

When that shot went through the hoop, I felt as if we'd somehow become invincible. There was no way any Garfield guy was going to muscle us, no way they were going to get one loose ball, or one contested rebound. No way.

For the next two minutes we totally shut Garfield down. A blocked shot. A double-team leading to a travel, a bounce pass out of bounds. A steal. We rattled them good, and on the offensive end, we made them pay for every mistake. I swished an eighteen-footer, Carver banked home a runner, Trent snaked in a finger roll off a drive to the hoop. The nine-teen-point lead was down to eleven.

Garfield's coach called time-out. It was so loud it was hard to hear anything O'Leary said. But what did it matter? We all knew what we had to do. Shut them down; score fast and often.

After the time out, Garfield went into a weave offense, try-ing to run us ragged and run time off the clock. There's no shot clock in Washington high school basketball, so you can stall as long as you want, and if the weave works you get a high-percentage shot.

But it only works if the defense goes to sleep. That pos-session was a war of wills. Who would crack first? Would it be one of us, going for the steal when it wasn't there and giving up the back-door lay-in? Or would it be one of them, a bad pass or a turnover on the dribble?

They had quickness, and all five of them could handle the ball. Ten seconds went off the clock. Twenty. Thirty. Then came the break. A bounce pass came low, hitting the guy I was guarding in the knee. In a flash I was down on the floor after it. The Garfield guy leaned over to tie me up, but before he could, I rolled the ball to McShane. Carver had broken free; McShane baseballed a pass the length of the court. Too high and too far—but Darren soared to catch it and in one motion put up a shot before tumbling out-of-bounds.

The shot was too hard. A Garfield guy was positioned for the rebound, but somehow it was Trent's hand that rose above his to tip the miss back up. The ball hung on the rim for an excruciating second. Two thousand people held their breath. And then it dropped in, and the place exploded. Again. The lead was only nine.

Right then we relaxed. It was only for a second, but we paid for it. Nobody had gotten back on defense. The in-bound went the length of the court to a streaking Garfield guard. He caught it, laid the ball up and in, and was fouled. When the free throw rattled in, their lead was twelve.

From that point on we were playing against the clock as much as we were playing against Garfield. They scored and then, but nothing they did—passing, shooting, rebounding— was crisp. They short-armed their shots and had rubbery knees on defense.

Everybody contributed. McShane rebounded like a demon. Luke made a beautiful cross on a drive up the gut and spun in a reverse lay-in. Carver swished a fifteen-footer with a hand in his face. I knocked down a sweeping hook from the right of the key. With two minutes and ten seconds left we pulled within five.

"De-fense! De-fense! De-fense!"

The crowd was up on its feet, exhorting us. I could feel another turnover coming. I could just feel it. Then, out of nowhere, their point guard rose and made a three-pointer from the corner even though I had my hand right in his face, and I mean right in his face. The lead jumped back to eight.

I rushed down court, determined to get the hoop back right away. But I was in too much of a hurry. I dribbled the ball off my knee, Garfield, picked it up, and they were off. As I watched that fast break develop, my heart stopped. Another bucket and they'd be up by ten and we'd be out of time.

I don't know how Trent got back, and I'm not sure his feet were really set. But he took the Garfield guy's knee in the chest, toppled backwards, and the ref bought it. "Offensive!" he shouted, and he pointed dramatically that the ball was to go our way.

At our end we worked the ball to Luke. His jumper was partially deflected. The rebound was one of those weird things that comes straight down. A pack of guys went for it, but the ball came out in McShane's possession. No hesitation—he went right back up with it and banked in a four-foot shot. We were down six with just over a minute left.

We pressed—no choice. But Garfield's point guard busted across the center line with a three-on-two fast break. He should have taken it to the basket, but he pulled it back to run the clock. The ball went down to the left corner. Trent and

Luke double-teamed, arms waving. The guy turned into Trent, and Trent yanked the ball out of his hands, just took it from him. I was off, and the pass was on the money. A Garfield guy planted himself at the top of the key. I wrapped the ball behind my back and blew by him. A simple lay-in, just like a million others I'd made. I laid the ball softly against the backboard and it settled into the net. Four down with fifty-three seconds left.

They brought the ball in before we could set up any kind of a press. And once they crossed the time-line they went into the four corners, spreading the court and making it impossible to double-team. Pass and cut, pass and cut, pass and cut. The seconds ticked away. When to foul? When to foul? I was about to hack at my guy when a pass slipped through the hands of their forward. Carver pounced on it, hit me, and we were off again. This time two guys were back. I drove into the lane, then skipped a pass to Carver. He was fifteen feet out and he stroked it, a beautiful jumper that was perfect. Down two with twenty seconds left.

O'Leary called time-out. "Go for a quick steal, but foul when it gets under fifteen. And remember—we have no more time-outs!"

The horn sounded. We turned and took the court. I was so tense I didn't hear the crowd, though they must have been screaming their lungs out. I couldn't swallow; there was no saliva in my mouth. I looked at Darren, at Luke, at McShane. They were as tight as I was. Then I looked at Trent. His eyes were glowing, that little crooked smile on his lips. All of a sudden my nervousness was gone. This was it—what I'd dreamed about for years. I might as well enjoy it.

We tried to deny the in-bound pass, but their center came back to get it. He returned the ball to the point guard, then set a solid screen as the guard worked the ball across the time line. With every dribble, a precious second ticked away.

Was it time to foul or was it still too early? I wanted to look at the clock, but I was afraid to take my eyes off my guy. Another dribble... another. I had to foul... I had to! But my guy got rid of the ball a fraction of a second before I could hack him. Right then our crowd picked up the clock. *Ten*... Luke was all over his guy. Still no call. *Nine*... A pass toward the top of the key. *Eight... Seven....* Another pass, this time cross-court. Time seemed to stop as the ball floated in the air. If it reached the Garfield guy deep in the corner, it was all over. We'd be out of time. I saw Darren dive, his fingertips stretching, stretching toward the ball, his body parallel to the ground. For an instant everything stopped — and then his hand was on the ball, tapping it away from the Garfield guy and toward me, and the world went from slow-motion to fast forward. In a flash I pounced on the ball, and broke for our hoop. I could hear the crowd counting down the seconds.... *Five... four...*

The guy guarding me had good position; I couldn't risk a charge, couldn't shoot over him. I looked left; Luke was covered. On the right I spotted Trent, but two Garfield guys were running stride-for-stride with him. I knew Darren was lying in a heap at the other end of the court. There was only one player left.

I penetrated the key while the crowd roared *Two*, then

spun and hit McShane as he spotted up just outside the three-point arc. It was his first three-point shot of the season. He released the ball as the crowd roared *One*. The shot was ugly—no arc, no spin, a laser. It streaked on a line to the backboard, smacked hard off the glass, and rocketed down and through the net just as the horn sounded.

The whole place gasped. It was as if no one believed what they'd just seen—the shot was so improbable. There was no way it could go in, but it had. McShane raised his arms above his head, and a huge smile spread across his face. A second later Luke tackled him, and everybody else piled on, until we must have looked like some ugly sea creature with more arms and legs than anyone could count.

Finally we stood, and arm-in-arm, danced our way off the court. From the stands poured down the most wonderful words in the world, wonderful because at least for that one moment they were true: "We're number one!"

Inside the locker room we hugged and high-fived, drummed on the benches and pounded on the metal lockers. We whooped and hollered as we showered, bouncing our excitement off the tile walls and floor.

You can't stay sky-high forever, though. The hot water changed to warm, then to cool. One by one guys turned off the water and headed back to the lockers.

As we dressed, guys broke into smaller groups. Still it was all the game—the drives to the hoop, the defensive stops, the baskets, the rebounds, McShane's incredible shot. Finally the talk wore down. Lockers banged closed; bags were zipped shut. Chang was the first one to leave, followed by Carver and Markey. "Great game!"..."See you Monday.".... "Later." One by one they left until it was just Trent and me.

"You in any big hurry?" he said.

I looked toward the door, thought about all the things that were outside it, all the things waiting for him and for me.

"No," I said. "Not really."

He shook his head. "Me neither."

So the two of us stayed where we were. A minute went by, then another, and another. It was pleasant just to sit, not saying anything.

Finally I stood. "Well, I guess we've got to go sometime, don't we?"

"Yeah. I guess we do."

We walked down the corridor. When we reached the door, I pushed it open. "Go ahead," I said.

He stepped outside and I followed.

The sun wasn't exactly out, but the sky wasn't all gray, either.

"Not a bad-looking day," I said.

"No," Trent answered, "not bad at all."